DEATH

The power of a SIG 226 .45 automatic

With a sneer of contempt, the badass unleathered a camofinished SIG 226 .45 automatic and levelled it point-blank at Trench's face. From this close up, even he couldn't miss.

The punk never got a chance to squeeze the trigger. Before the breakpoint came and the hammer fell hard on the chambered round, Trench's UZI spoke. The point-blank headshot disintegrated the top of the wheelman's skull, popping the eyeballs from their sockets. . .

PHOENIX

GROUND ZERO
David Alexander

A STAR BOOK
published by
the Paperback Division of
W. H. Allen & Co. Plc

A Star Book
Published in 1988
by The Paperback Division of
W. H. Allen & Co. Plc
44 Hill Street, London W1X 8LB

First published by
Dorchester Publishing Co. Inc. in 1987

Printed and bound in Great Britain by
Anchor Brendon Ltd, Tiptree, Essex

ISBN 0 352 32170 9

Man is but a reed, the most feeble thing in nature; but he is a thinking reed. The entire universe need not arm itself to crush him; a vapor, a drop of water suffice to kill him. But when the universe has crushed him, man will still be nobler than that which kills him, because he knows that he is dying, and of its victory the universe knows nothing.

—Pascal, *Pensees*

"Tell me about the rabbits, George."

—Steinbeck, *Of Mice and Men*

PROLOGUE

Crimson spouted from the shattered base of the skull as a longburst of 185-grain HV steel-jacketed wadcutters screaming from a Steyr MPi69 SMG outfitted with a SIONICS silencer struck the target's skull, buzzsawing it into a thousand jagged fragments.

The headless corpse pitched crazily forward. Its weapon, an Uzi .45 ACP Micro, clattered from lifeless fingers. Brain-matter cocktail slopped from the open chalice of the skull, spattering the dirty boots. The corpse lurched onto its knees, then keeled over on its side. Firing nerve ends jerked the legs and arms of the torso, giving it the appearance of some gigantic earthworm as it crawled forward leaving a trail of bloody slime.

The killforcer spun fast as another target entered his performance envelope. A MAC 11 SMG in the target's hand sang a lethal death-song, spitting out 230-grain roundnose whizzers at 700 rounds per minute. The black Z-Coated weapon belched in the fastgunner's fist, sounding a full-auto death knel as a figure-six fragburst of whirlwinding hollowpoints scythed into this new threat's chest cavity, producing a tight, symmetrical shot pattern.

Bullet fragments liquified the colon and liver to a bloody soup as they buzzed around inside the chest cavity like angry steel hornets. Chunks of the heart and right lung adhering to a glob consisting of muscle tissue, still twitching as it was torn loose from bone and ligament, sailed through the air.

Another corpse pitched forward, writhing where it fell as blood pooled around its chest.

A deadly blossom of white-hot flame spouted as fast-cycling 9-mm autofire was directed at the man in the black bodysuit from two directions at once. The withering cross fire would have severed another man in two at the belt line, but the fastgunner did a dive and somersault just as the blazing stitches converged, followed by a tuck and roll that brought him beyond the fire zone's lethal perimeter.

He came up firing at one of the heavily armed targets with the Steyr SMG while his free hand whipped a ballistic knife from a fast-draw sheath on his upper left thigh and aimed it at the second attacker with the precision of a missile-tracking computer array.

Autofire seemed to pour from the weapon's superheated muzzle in a molten stream, directed with pinpoint accuracy in a zigzag configuration that hacked the first attacker's head and upper torso to bloody pieces and hurled them against the cinderblock wall.

A ballistic knife blade was propelled 30 feet as the spring in its handle violently uncoiled, to lodge deeply in the stomach of the second attacker. The man threw his arms up as he pitched backward, his SMG chattering briefly as death spasms jerked the trigger finger, then sprawled on the bloodstained concrete with his head turned completely around, his neck snapped like a dry twig.

Bright light suddenly impaled the survivor in the darksuit like a wasp on a glittering pin. The fastgunner faced into the glare, seeing nothing but the brightness lancing through the velveteen blackness beyond. Clear and cold, a voice rang out from the tiers above the arena in which he stood.

The voice told the fastgunner that he would continue to live. If he would make a pact.

A pact of steel.

Then the light snapped off and the fastgunner stood again in semidarkness. When his vision had again adjusted, he was alone in the vast arena, surrounded by the mangled corpses of the men he'd just killed.

A steel-plate door slid noiselessly on hidden tracks, allowing the victor egress from the death-trap that had claimed a dozen lives in as many minutes.

Before turning to leave, the man in the dark-suit noticed for the first time, in the spill of light from the sterile corridor beyond the killground, that the targets seemed all to have been similar in build, as though they had all been deliberately selected on the basis of that resemblance. Something else he noticed convinced him of this.

Above the heart of each of the corpses was a tattoo. It was the tattoo of a bird with spread wings, rising skyward above licking tongues of fire which tried in vain to consume it.

The fastgunner spun on his heels and left the arena. He did not give another thought to what he had seen. Everything, he was certain, would be explained to him in time.

BOOK ONE

IN LIKE A LION

1

For a long time Trinity had been—and now was even more so—a ghost town. It was situated on the sunbaked anvil of the Black Rock Desert of northwestern Nevada. Rich lodes of gold, silver, and iron ore had been discovered there in the early 1900s.

For almost 30 years, before the lodes dried up, Trinity had been home of some of the baddest desperadoes in the West. Gunfights on its dusty main street were as common in Trinity as handshakes were elsewhere. Cathouses, gambling halls, and saloons flourished and their proprietors became wealthy overnight while prospectors and grubstakers carted away over $250 million in gold from Trinity's rich mines.

It took nuclear hellfire to make Trinity live again—even if its inhabitants still were ghosts. The squatters who repopulated the town, extending its boundaries well into the desert in an ever-widening radius, were the brutal remnants of post-World-War-III America who had fled the burning cities into the badlands of the desert wastes to live or die in a world of dog-eat-dog and man-kill-man.

There were towns like Trinity scattered all across the ruined hellscape of America, courtesy of the same people who had brought it social chaos, mutant-causing Plague, and nuclear megadeaths. Brawling freeholds for rootless bands of pathetic survivors who had sunk down to, and in many cases below, the level of primitive savagery. Places where anything could be bought or sold or traded if the price were right and the buyer's need were great enough.

Unlike the others, though, Trinity had a single distinction to make its name worthy of remembrance.

It was visited briefly by Magnus Trench, the man called Phoenix.

Trench had fled the SCORF attack squad with the beautiful September Song, leaving the damned of San Francisco to make it or break it in the toxic hellhole the Bay City had become. In the San Joaquin Valley, the blue-eyed daughter of an American G.I. and a Vietnamese whore had chosen to stay with a commune made up of survivors from the nuke-scorched ruins of Los Angeles and Trench had gone on alone, outfitting himself with a turbocharged Camaro XL-69 to replace the stolen military vehicle he'd ridden in on.

From there, he'd skirted the slaughterhouse of Los Angeles, riding hard along Route 15 on a course he hoped would keep him away from the worst danger zones of social upheaval and chemonuclear contamination as he roared through the Western states toward New York City.

There he would move hell and earth to discover if Sandra and Brian, his wife and son, were still numbered among the living. If they were, then somehow Trench would see to it that the three of them would survive the nuclear nightmare of World War III. If not, then the Dark Messiah and his puppet U.S. Government would discover that their nightmare was only now beginning.

Trinity lay just off Interstate 95, cluttered with dead and rusting vehicles containing picked-clean corpses and patrolled by badass rip squads, but still navigable. At night, the town's lights were an eerily flickering glow against the horizon line.

Trench urgently needed gas and food. Armed with the "Megastopper," a lightweight yet lethal MINIMI M249 machine gun with a 40-round clip of BTHP 235-grain hollowpoints, and two .45 ACP Micro Uzi SMGs dangling from each arm on fast-grab lanyards ready for instant deployment, the massively muscled warrior rated instant attention and respect as he passed beneath the crudely lettered wooden sign into the town's crowded center.

"Blue Ecstacy Job, mister?" a whore with a row of bleached-blonde spikes growing out of her otherwise cleanly shaven skull, wearing thigh-high boots and a black-leather bodysuit that left her pussy, butt, and breasts exposed, pro-positioned, frankly offering her long silver-painted nipples. "Check out the goods."

She bent over and spread the cheeks of her ass. "I'll take 'em as big as they come."

"Dust, crack, smoke . . . young boys . . ." another hustler on Trinity's main drag chanted in a dull monotone. ". . . acid, SPASM, smack, coke . . ."

"Long pig?" a bald dwarf with Plague pustules on his face asked. His breath was rank as he grabbed Trench by the elbow. "Butchered fresh today. You get to crack open the skull, spoon out the brains. Builds your body against the Plague. Tastes good too. Whaddaya say, chief?" Trench booted the dwarf aside. He flopped on his face into the dust and got up shaking his tiny fist and shouting unflattering things about Trench's mother.

A forest of hostile eyes tracked Trench, but nobody made a move. Even the most unreceptive could see it was bad karma to mess with the heavy-metal-wielding doomsman in their midst.

A fat woman with one half of her face lost beneath a mass of pus-oozing blisters and the other painted gold was hawking "desert buck" out of a fairway stall. Drawing closer, Trench saw the carcasses of skinned dogs hanging from the stall's front. Across from the stall was a whip-seller's store where a live model, twisted into a torture position resembling an upside-down parrot chained to its perch, hung over the doorway. Trench turned his attention back to the woman at the "desert buck" stall.

"What's today's special?" Phoenix asked.

"Desert buck fricassee on a stick," she replied. "Got some hot ones on the grill. Try one, friend? Only five n-bucks each."

Trench glared at the proprietress. "How much did you say?"

She cleared her throat. "For friends, fifty cents." Trench nodded. The dogmeat was a greasy blob skewered on an ice-cream stick. "Who runs this place?" he asked the woman as he tore off a piece of the fried dog.

"Maybe I can be of service," said a voice from behind him before the woman could reply. The voice belonged to a scav geek with a bullet head and an eye patch, wearing black-leather jeans and a black-leather vest open to expose a well-muscled chest.

It was not the face or the voice of a man any reasonably sane person would be prone to trust on sight. "My name is Dart, short for D'Artagnan. The man you need is called Electric Larry. I can take you to him."

Dart extended a hand the size of a dinner plate. His glittering black eyes briefly flitted to the tattoo of the Phung Hoang—the mark of the Vietnamese Phoenix that Trench had received in the steaming jungles of Southeast Asia what seemed like a million years ago—above Trench's heart. When Trench shook hands, he applied enough pressure to make Dart's eyes bug.

"Sure," he returned. "Show me to the man."

Dart led him through a maze of badass-thronged streets to a deserted area behind some shacks. Trench could feel the bushwhack attempt before it happened. It wasn't even worth wasting ammo on. Two guys came down from the surrounding rooftops. Both wielded knives and tried real hard to look menacing.

Trench took out the shivmen with a series of Laughing Crane kicks that first shattered their arms and then their breastbones. As the bodies fell to the ground and did a last-gasp boogaloo, Dart came at him with a gravity blade and a smile on his face. Trench blocked the lunge, disarmed the would-be bushwhacker, and laid him out with blood pouring out of Dart's busted face. Dart wasn't smiling anymore as Trench hauled the big guy to his feet one-handed.

"You gonna take me to the man or what?" he intoned.

Dart's blood-spitting gurgle was the hurried assent of a man suddenly convinced of his own mortality.

"Uh-huh..." said the short guy named Hendrix to his partner, a hulking dude in a black-leather cowboy hat and brown-suede jacket. "We got a definite reading on that one, Reaperman."

In the short man's hand was a CAM, or Chemical Agent Monitor. It resembled a portable utility flashlight, with a handle grip above a stubby rectangular housing, except that, where a flashlight had a flaring lens, the CAM had a tapering sensor bulb calibrated to electronically "sniff" trace quantities of various substances on surfaces or in ambient air.

Above the sensor tip was a microprocessor-driven LED readout which displayed information on substance concentration on a bar graph and responded with a series of audible tones for a directional fix on the source.

Programmed by a snap-in module, the CAM was now electronically configured to recognize the odor of the toluene tri-paradioxin or TTBP molecule. This molecule was present only in the cells of humans resistant to the TTBP Plague, which, as a result of Russian NBC warfare, had turned a large percentage of the population into Contams—soulless mutant killers with a thirst for blood and a hunger for human flesh, walking cancers whose illness made them bloodthirsty zombies.

Those resistant to the Plague were Immunes, and were wanted dead or alive by the Government for a crash program to counter the disease. While approximately 15 percent of the post-nuclear population of the United States were Immunes, there was only one Immune-Alpha—a human containing antibodies to the Plague which destroyed it on contact—discovered so far. That man was Magnus Trench, the man called Phoenix.

Even for humans who had not contracted the Plague, Cesium 137 filtering down from the upper atmosphere created long-term genetic damage.

And UV radiation spilling through giant holes ripped by nuclear warfare in the Earth's ozone layer burned and disfigured the greater percentage of people no matter what.

Immune bounty hunters roved through the wasteland of America, searching for their human prey for big bucks from Luther Enoch's new but not improved Uncle Sam. They were heavily armed, and their quarry seldom escaped—at least not alive.

"That big hombre up ahead," Hendrix returned with a nervous tremor in his voice as he stared at the readout in disbelief. "We're getting Alpha readings, Reaperman."

"The walking arsenal?" the goliath hunter, Reaperman, asked. "You sure, man?" Hendrix nodded. The CAM readout was flashing the body specs of the Immune: weight, 250 pounds; height, six feet, two inches; antibody concentration, ultra-high. The readings indicated that this Immune was a veritable white whale of antibodies. Hendrix had never seen readings so phenomenally high.

Reaperman cocked the bolt on his Skorpion MK18 SMG, jacking a 9-mm round into the chamber. He turned toward the hunters behind him, similarly armed with automatic weapons. Using hand signals, Reaperman indicated the man moving through the crowd toward Trinity's gate.

"Show time," he saidd. "Let's stick it to the fucker."

Phoenix strode through the swarm of tight-packed bodies down Trinity's main drag on his way out of town. As far as he was concerned, five seconds in that hellhole was enough to make him sick to his stomach, and he'd already spent a lot more time than that.

Once Dart and his punks had been put out of commission, Electric Larry had been willing to deal. Trench now had two ten-gallon plastic cans of high octane dangling from his shoulders and a haversack full of such delicacies as German shepherd stuffed with rice and fillet of ground hog. As soon as he got to his wheels and gassed up, he was out of that scum burg.

The ambush went down as Phoenix cleared Trinity's fairgrounds, leaving the most crowded sections behind. Three bounty hunters had taken the lead with another four coming up behind. They had him bracketed on both sides.

"All right, hernia bag—freeze and live! Twitch and we smoke you."

The center badass was pointing a big, mean matte-black SPAS-12 combat shotgun directly at him. The gun was a cannon. At point-blank range, there wouldn't be enough left to put between two hamburger buns—providing you could find any hamburger buns, that is. The other two punks pointed SMGs of various types and calibers and grinned wide like mules with bellyfuls of shit.

Trench dove, avoiding a lethal cross fire that caught the badasses on either end across the belly, Swiss-cheesing them instantly. Hunkering behind a fairground stall, he took cover as autofire shattered glass and molten lead whizzed around his body like a hailstorm in hell, snapping the first steel-jacketed wadcutter round into the Megastopper's chamber.

Autofire from the clip-fed MINIMI M249 lifted a pair of hunter-killer punks off their feet and sent them back to earth with their bodies torn open in a dozen places. Steel-jacketed .45 ACP slugs razored through flesh, muscle, and bone, leaving ugly hunks of raw, bloody hamburger showing through the huge gashes in their stomachs and chests. But there were more hunters coming in to take the dead men's places. And some of Trinity's braver denizens, smelling a profitable hustle going down, were breaking from the sidelines to get in on the action.

In under five minutes, almost the entire town of Trinity seemed to be firing at Trench, sensing a buck to be made at the expense of one of the most worthless things in the nuke-blasted world: a human life. Trench could even see the bald dwarf who sold cannibal dinners he'd stiff-armed earlier blasting away on full-auto with an M16A42 assault rifle almost as big as he was.

There was only one way Phoenix would get his ass out of Trinity alive. And that meant using those two precious cans of gas he'd brought from Electric Larry.

Phoenix cut the rope securing both cans. Grabbing one severed rope end, he swung a gasoline can overhead and let it fly like a discus. The can hit the ground midway between his position and the badass homicide crew, mostly intact but with its plastic leaking fluid.

Just as fast, Trench launched the other can in the opposite direction. On the follow-through, he fisted both Micro UZI SMGs and fired twin fragbursts at each can.

The cans went up with a loud *whump* and twin blinding-yellow fireballs. Trench could feel the intense heat singing his eyeballs as two immense pillars of flame mushroomed skyward, creating a narrow corridor between them.

Bodies engulfed in flames, their centers black puppet figures swathed in licking, fiery curtains, lurched crazily through the corridor as they were burned alive. The heat ignited both the grenades they carried on military webbing and the ammo in their automatic weapons. The chaotic fireworks produced by these exploding munitions added to the diversion Trench had created. Death would be his ally, chaos his friend.

Trench let go of the Uzis and slammed a fresh clip into the M249. The compact MG spat deathfire from its bell-shaped muzzle as Trench hightailed it through the corridor, snapping off eight-round bursts to either side as he ran.

He couldn't see his car, but there was a Bronco four-by-four parked nearby. He climbed into the four-by-four and hot-wired the engine. The powerful overhead-cam V-8 roared to life as Trench threw the muscle cruiser into gear and burned rubber onto the highway. Against hope and against sanity there was the slim chance that he would make it out of Trinity without further opposition.

But his hope was short-lived.

Out of the dense smoke obscuring Trinity came a wave of pursuit cars, screaming off after the fleeing Bronco in a high-velocity death chase.

2

The speedometer needle shot past the redline and went off the scale. Four hundred horses under the Bronco's hood galloped full tilt into the open mouth of hell as the fat-wheeled muscle cruiser roared through the miles of red sand and craggy cliffs called the Desert of Fire.

Behind the escape car sped an assortment of pursuit vehicles ranging from long-bed pickups to motorcycle-sidecar combos.

Most of Trinity was now hot-wheeled hell screaming off in pursuit of the big stranger with the deadly firepower.

Trench tapped the Bronco's gas gauge. The needle was frozen in position. No way to tell if he had a full tank or was just riding on his fumes.

Something moved in the seat behind him. Trench caught the flicker in the reflective surface of the dashboard gauges. Before he could react, cold steel was jammed into the back of his head.

Trench could see the gaunt, sallow face in the rearview mirror. The cold black eyes peered over the long black barrel of a Colt Python .357 magnum. This kind of trouble Trench needed like a . . . he stopped himself from thinking "like a hole in the head."

The line wasn't clever and it sure wasn't funny, especially considering he was a heartbeat away from becoming mostly hole and very little head. Another glance at the sideview told him that the trigger-happy townspeople of Trinity were getting dangerously close.

Trench's mind raced. He'd have one shot and one shot only. The Python's length could be his way out. Long-barreled weapons in close quarters were easy to grab—the hard part came after you grabbed them and they went off in your face.

"Looks like I woke up into your nightmare, puppy dog," said the goon pointing the iron his way. "You pull this rig over right now or your ass ain't a pisshole in the sand."

"And if I don't?" Trench asked. The dude's breath was something somebody should have told him about. Dog meat and cheap wine were an unhealthy combination.

"At this range, I expect that means most of your head goes through the windshield."

"At this speed, you die too," Trench reminded the cancer-faced geek.

"I'm willing to take the chance," returned the ugly. The eyes in the rearview flicked left. "Over—"

The momentary eye movement was enough for Trench. It *had* to be. With a swift backlash of his free right arm, he grabbed the Colt's long barrel, holding its muzzle away from his head. The big .44-caliber mag discharged through the Bronco's roof as the badass jerked the Colt's hair trigger.

On the follow-through, Trench's elbow smashed into the badguy's jaw so hard the punk's head crashed through the window.

Steering one-handed, Phoenix reached around and booted the hardcase out the door. The corpse did a roll-and-bounce, then rag-dolled out across the highway, as dead as they came.

The fight had cost Trench precious seconds, seconds in which the motorized murder crew was rapidly bringing the Bronco into range of their gunsights.

In the lead were two four-by-fours driven by the surviving bounty hunters. The hardriders in both were armed with grenades, FFV LAW AT4 rockets, SMGs, and Valmet-AK-series automatic assault rifles. More important, they were professionals who would keep on coming until they either came out winners or came out dead.

"Can't you get any more speed out of this rust-bucket?" the hunter in the shotgun seat asked the wheelman, a shirtless dude with a giant scorpion tattooed on his skinny, sweaty chest and belly. "We gotta take this creep out. It's bad business if we don't."

Reaperman scowled as he watched the Bronco kick up clouds of pale desert dust.

"Hey, I'm giving her all she's got!" the wheelman shot back. "You wanna wind up all over the landscape, Reaperman, or what?"

"Use the fuckin' nitrogen fuel injectors!" the bounty hunter screamed at the sweat-soaked wheelman.

"But—"

"*No buts!*" Reaperman jammed his MK18's short barrel into the wheelman's side, flat against the ribs showing through the papery flesh like umbrella spars. "Now, jerkwad!"

The wheelman shrugged and pulled back the knob releasing the super-rich mixture into the cruiser's carb. The RAM 350 lurched from side to side as it surged forward with the sound of screaming metal and burning rubber while the enriched octane mixture revved the V-8's pistons to twice their rated performance levels, moving from 100 mph to close to 150 in just under five seconds.

Heavy-duty Michelin steel-belted radials spun so fast they left smoking black treadmarks behind as the muscle cruiser tore up the highway at three times the double nickel, closing the gap between it and the bucking Bronc escape car in less time than it takes to say a prayer.

Hell screamed from the 9-mm Skorpion belching flame from the fastgunner's fist as Reaperman hung out the RAM's door with the wind whipping back his long hair and his features twisted into a hideous fright mask of primitive fury.

"Whoo-eee!" he screamed.

"*Eat shit, maggot!*"

HP wadcutters slammed the blacktop at 1100 feet per second, kicking up a line of high-flying asphalt chunks inches behind the fleeing four-by-four's rear fender.

Phoenix had seen the chase car close the gap with deathfire vomiting from it and had brought one of the small yet deadly Micro Uzi SMGs into position for backhanded firing out the Bronco's window. He'd half expected that at least one of those goons in the chase cars had rigged up a nitrogen supercharger. If Trench could just manage to hold his lead, he still had a snowball's chance, but with the gas gauge frozen, who knew how long he could maintain the critical edge?

Trench blind-fired his Uzi at the four-by-four as it pulled up close. Bullets from the chase car's chattering MK18 SMG crossed the Uzi's kill path in a lethal cross fire, shattering the Bronco's rear

windshield and spanging off the four-by-four's
fender. The chase car swerved wildly to avoid
being stitched by Uzi fire.

But there was double trouble bringing up the
rear. From the opposite end, the second of the
four-by-fours leading the pursuing rat pack was
edging slightly behind the lead car. Phoenix went
into a series of tail-wagging evasive zigzags that,
for the moment, minimized his chances of a direct
hit in a fatal area, but that wouldn't work forever.

The automatic-armed killgunner reloaded as
the lead-chase-car wheelman brought the road-
hugging four-by-four almost abreast of Trench's
muscle cruiser. Trench could see the hardguy in
the shotgun seat snap a fresh clip into his weapon
with a fluid movement and jerk the short, ugly
snout of the Skorpion into position for a headshot. The bounty hunter was missing an ear and
had a tuft of greasy black hair sprouting from the
side of a cueball skull. Reaperman flipped Trench
the bird just before he pulled the MK18's trigger.

Trench swung the Uzi over and blasted the
ugly's face. Mixmastered brains shot into orbit
but only got as high as the RAM's roof. Bullet
fragments passed through the spurting visceral
pulp, deflecting off bone into the wheelman's
chest cavity, puncturing the heart and lungs and
immediately drowning the wheelman in his own
blood.

The four-by-four lurched and peeled off the
roadway as Trench's Bronco nudged ahead of the
stricken pursuit vehicle. It crashed into the
concrete median, splitting in two, spun and
turned end-over-end, then burst into flames.
Pieces of flash-fried corpses took wing for rat
heaven as the gas tank blew and a long column of
thick black smoke erupted in a ball of incandescent yellow-white flame that licked at

the sky's soft blue belly.

Bounty hunters in the second four-by-four narrowly avoided hitting the out-of-control death-trap the RAM had become, but lost ground to Trench's escape car. The fastgunner in the second RAM was taking no chances here. The situation called for heavier firepower and subzero cool.

The second fastgunner whipped out a LAW rocket launcher and flipped off the protective caps at either end. Retracting the trigger guard, he armed the rocket inside. Standing up and sighting through the RAM's sun roof, the badman let fly his anti-armor predator bird, his vision momentarily obscured by a pall of dense gray smoke produced by the rocket's exhaust.

Trench swerved just in time to avoid the explosion as the lethal warhead slammed into the roadside to his left. The detonation's impact rocked his four-by-four, blowing off the Bronco's hubcaps and propelling its left wheels off the ground before they grabbed blacktop again.

"Damn that bastard!" the hunter swore, pulling a grenade from his belt as he flung the now-useless and still-smoking launcher out the window. "Pour some RPMs into this shitpile and bring me up to that cocksucker!"

The second four-by-four pulled almost even with Trench on the passenger side of the highway. The wheelman was good, managing to jockey up against the Bronc even with Trench zigzagging the wheel and wiggling his ass to give his pursuers almost no maneuvering room to pass.

"Bye bye, fuckhead!" the hardman screamed as he pulled the cotter pin securing the grenade's spoon-locking mechanism free, and grasped it tightly prior to lobbing it in through the window.

Trench fired a one-handed Uziburst,

temporarily losing steering control but choosing between the lesser of two evils. Hit by a brace of .45 ACP wadcutters, the RAM wheelman brought his hands to his face. But there was no face left by the time they got there. Most of it was sticking to the shattered windshield, except the left eye, which hung from the rearview by a fibrous cord of nerve tissue.

The RAM swerved crazily, broadsiding the Bronco as Trench fought the wheel for control at the same instant the fastgunner let go of the ticking grenade. The grenade dropped between the fastgunner's legs and rolled under the seat. The three guys left in the truck dodged the kicking feet of the headless corpse as they frantically groped for the dropped grenade while Trench's Bronco pulled ahead.

"I got it!" one of the goon guys yelled, just as the grenade ignited with a deafening roar, blowing the roof off the cruiser and sending it and the three passengers—now in several sloppy pieces—30 feet into the air.

Eating up blacktop, Trench saw the second wave of pursuit vehicles swerving desperately as they tried to avoid colliding with the crippled RAM, the burning remains of which were raining down across the highway from three separate directions as flaming body parts fell like barbecue from heaven.

There was no way most could apply the brakes in time to avoid the massive, deadly pileup that resulted when successive skids and crashes turned the blacktop into an obstacle course for the vehicles careening toward the jagged flying metal at breakneck speeds.

A skidding pickup was struck with buzz-sawing metal debris that crashed through its windshield and severed its wheelman's head. The pickup became an incandescent sunball as its fuel lines ruptured and caught fire. Flailing like snakes, bodies flew from its open bed and cascaded onto the desert to feed the worms and the maggots. Unable to stop in time, a trio of hard-riding bikers crashed into the wall of flame. The bikes went sailing into space. Midway up, the riders separated from them. The bodies landed broken and mangled beyond recognition.

But Trench wasn't out of the woods yet. Not by a longshot.

There was still a final wave of cars that had—through skill, blind luck, or a combination of both—managed to avoid the flaming pileup on the highway to hell. They had lost time by swerving off the blacktop and onto the desert-scape on either side, but they were still solidly behind Trench. In seconds, they'd gain enough ground to put Phoenix in range of their guns.

Sure enough, a Blazer long-bed cruiser riding on high-mag wheels ate up the gap in seconds. Fiery roses blossomed in the muzzles of Demro WASP SMGs as frag slugs shattered glass and slammed into the Bronco's dashboard, narrowly avoiding ripping a hole in Trench's skull. It looked like a whole family of badasses was using him for target practice.

Autofire was ratcheting not only from the cab, but from a bunch of uglies on the truck bed as well. Phoenix made a mental note to keep far away from Trinity if he ever got out of this hellstorm alive, the prospects of which seemed less and less likely as the Blazer pulled abreast of Trench's highballing Bronco.

Then the worst happened.

The Bronco's engine suddenly began to die as the cylinders succumbed to metal fatigue like heart tissue undergoing cardiac arrest. Dense gray smoke billowed in acrid clouds from beneath the hood as the four-by-four lost velocity.

The Blazer was edging up closer. A locust swarm of molten lead was flying at him from both its cab and its bed. He could see the smiles break out as the crew in the Blazer watched his four-by-four slow noticeably. They knew they had the dude dead-bang and were already counting the money the Immune's corpse would bring them.

Once more, Trench's Uzi spoke and a hail of lead took out the fastgunner in the Blazer's cab before he could reload. That left the wheelman and the four other duds on the truck bed. Trench unhooked an antipersonnel grenade from his belt and waited till the Blazer's rear drew parallel to the Bronco's cab, then pitched it, goosing the Bronco ahead. As the grenade blew, the Blazer wheelman aimed his weapon across the corpse of his former pard in the shotgun seat. Trench pulled back just as a 9-mm burst pounded hell out of the Bronco's windshield, showering him with fragments of safety glass.

It was now or never.

Fighting the incredible wind resistance, Trench ripped open the driver's side door and leaped from the stricken Bronco onto the pickup's bed. The corpses on the deck cushioned the impact of landing. He dropped the MINIMI to give himself swinging room and moved toward the cab.

The snout of a MAC-11 appeared and Trench ducked as deathfire whipsawed through a section of air he'd just stood in. The wheelman might have been an ace driver, but he was an amateur when it came to guns. Firing a longburst from the fast-cycling MAC had emptied the clip in two seconds flat. Before the wheelman could feed the MAC another clip, Phoenix lunged around the side of the Blazer's cab in an attempt to grab the wheelman by the throat and yank him out of the cruiser.

Luck was temporarily on the punk's side. Fear abetted his automatic reflexes and the wheelman whacked Trench in the face with the stock of the Ingram, momentarily blinding him. He kept clubbing Trench until the bloodied fingers lost their grip on the edge of the truck and the ferocious wind resistance did the rest.

The wheelman laughed sadistically as Trench disappeared from sight. He looked back, anxious to see the mangled body rolling broken on the highway in the truck's fast-moving slipstream.

3

The wheelman's smile quickly turned down at the corners when he didn't see any mangled corpse rolling in the Blazer's slipstream. No, he thought to himself. It couldn't be. Or could it?

Maybe it *was* impossible.

But that didn't mean you couldn't do it if your life depended on it.

Grabbing the undercarriage, Trench narrowly avoided getting creamed by the spinning wheels, his heels dragging over the speeding asphalt so rapidly they actually made sparks fly from his high black laceups.

The wheelman realized he had a passenger on his belly and began swerving crazily, intending to shake him off. Head reeling, Trench managed to swing both legs onto the sides of the camshaft housing and lock them into position. He shook his head to clear the blood from his eyes and inched around to the other side. Fighting the fierce wind resistance to climb back onto the truck bed, Trench tore at the passenger-side door, hoping it wasn't locked. Too bad for the wheelman it wasn't. The door flew open.

The sole of a booted foot slammed into Trench's face with a ferocious thrust kick as the driver saw the bloodied head appear in the open door framed against the dizzily speeding landscape. Keeping his left foot on the gas pedal, the wheelman prepared to finish the turkey off with a second headbuster stomp.

Before he had a chance to deliver the killing blow, Phoenix lashed out, catching the boot by the ankle and pulling with every ounce of force in his massive right arm. Clutching the steering wheel for dear life, the wheelman fishtailed crazily across the yellow line in an attempt to shake off the hell-vision. No guy *that* busted up could keep taking the punishment he was dishing out. Except that this dude was somehow doing exactly that.

The Blazer wheelman decided to just blow the sucker away.

With a sneer of contempt, the badass unleathered a camo-finished SIG 226 .45 automatic and leveled it point-blank at Trench's face. From this close up, even he couldn't miss.

The punk never got a chance to squeeze the trigger. Before the breakpoint came and the hammer fell hard on the chambered round, Trench's Uzi spoke. The point-blank headshot disintegrated the top of the wheelman's skull, popping the eyeballs from their sockets.

Death spasms jerked the wheel back and forth as the decorticated thing flung itself around the Blazer's cab. The body pitched forward after a few brief seconds, tripping the windshield wipers of the careening four-by-four and blaring the horn with its dead weight.

Shouldering the corpse out the driver's door, Trench took over the wheel and got the Blazer back under control. Coming up in the rearview he could see the last wave of chase cars. These were Trinity's dregs, driving beat-up old wrecks and using garbage weapons. They wouldn't be too hard to handle.

Trench reached for his leg holster and freed a lethal sidearm he'd picked up from the valley people. It was a Heckler-Koch 40-mm grenade-launching pistol. Finished in a glinting steel-blue, the parkerized weapon resembled a miniature cannon. A long, thin pop-up sight extended from the wide barrel and a retractable metal stock opened from the butt to steady the weapon, which was accurate at up to 1000 yards.

Stopping the four-by-four, Trench whipped open the driver's door and aimed the HK "Granatpistole" at the half-dozen vehicles arranged in a mobile wing formation. He could hear the distant rattle of autofire as they closed the mile-long gap between him and them. He steadied the sight on the point vehicle and fired.

A dead-on hit engulfed the point car in a yellow-orange fireball. It went up taking two on either side with it. Flaming debris spun and danced high in the air, before raining back down to earth in a slow pavane of burning metal and flesh. The bracket cars pulled up short. There was sporadic firing and then a lull.

Trench reloaded and sighted on a point midway between the two brackets.

Dead, frozen silence.

Then the inevitable happened. The surviving vehicles turned and drove off in the opposite direction, past the smoking piles of charred debris which were the remains of the cowboys who'd ridden out with them.

Smiling grimly, Trench let the second shell fly. It exploded on the tails of the remaining cars, though not close enough to do them any major damage.

It would be a sad night in Trinity for the chase's survivors.

Trench reholstered the HK grenade pistol in the custom speed rig on his thigh and leaned against the four-by-four. He rested the backs of his arms against the hot, dirt-caked metal. Then he moved into the back.

Two corpses remained on the truck bed. Phoenix cleared them off and left them for the buzzards. He retrieved his MINIMI and leaned the big, black licking stick against the side of the truck. When it came to a weapon like the Belgian-designed SAW weapon, Trench had one motto.

Don't leave hell without it.

Hostile eyes tracked him, and he wasn't even aware of it. Contams were in the hot sands, the victims of Plague-induced mutations created when the Soviet biological weapons had discharged their deadly cargo.

The genetic structure of the Plague showed similarities to the lentivirus family. Both caused chronic degenerative neurologic and structural changes in the victim.

Like AIDS, another lentivirus it closely resembled, the Plague virus breeched the blood-brain barrier, causing wide-ranging damage.

Neoplasms affected the brain and musculature, resulting in slobbering, submental idiocy combined with wildly uncontrolled physical growth, in many cases to the point of gigantism.

These Contams used mutant desert creatures to hunt with. They bred them. They had witnessed the fight.

Dug inside the burning sands until nightfall, when they would arise to begin their nocturnal hunting, the Contams feasted on the road kills which often littered the highways, finding them to be an excellent source of protein.

There were animals too, and in the absence of those, each other. To Contams anything, including themselves, was edible.

But the sound of the explosions rocking the soil had shaken them from their dreamless sleep. They smelled death in the air. They rose to take what they could before other scavengers beat them to the fresh road kills.

Trench alerted to the faint scraping sounds behind him. Swerving from the Blazer, he reacted with horror to what he saw.

The sand erupted as hideously deformed giants rose from fetal positions beneath the earth. He recognized them instantly as Contams. He had encountered these diseased mutants in Frisco. He watched horrified as they rose from the ground, like warriors sown from dragons' teeth.

In addition to the Contams, mutant desert creatures were also on the warpath. The Contams seemed to control them, using them as hunters use dogs to retrieve their prey. Trench braced for the attack.

A phalanx of Contams shambled toward him, snarling with rage, their eyes filled with hunger. Trench grabbed fistfuls of heavy metal and squeezed off twin longbursts in figure eights which cut down the mutant army and sent the others scattering out of harm's way.

Which was just as well, because he was down to his last ammo clip.

Slamming the cab door, Trench lobbed two of his last remaining grenades into the regrouping Contams. Tumerous flesh was pulped as the shrapnel and high explosive created a rain of body parts in the parched desertscape. Phoenix cranked the ignition key. The powerful engine roared to life.

And just as quickly died.

"Damn!" Trench cursed, trying the ignition again without success. The carb would be boiling over, he knew. Grabbing up the MINIMI, Trench climbed out the passenger-side door and crouched behind the cover of the fender. Lobbing another grenade, he scrambled for the safety of a rock out-cropping some hundred yards away.

For every Contam the pineapple trashed, there seemed to be a dozen more coming. Trench emptied the MINIMI's last remaining 40-round clip until the firing pin clicked on an empty chamber.

Trench grabbed the M249 by its barrel and swung it like a club. Brains shattered as mutants went down in sprawling heaps to either side.

As he reared back to take a killer swipe, a leprously scabbed hand crashed up out of the hot sand and grabbed his ankle. Another followed.

Scores of Contams closed in from every direction. The empty MINIMI MG was wrenched from his grasp and disappeared forever.

The sand beneath his feet gave way as hungry jaws opened below, pulling him down into a vortex of sand. He flailed desperately with his naked fists as Contams tried to bite off his face.

Trench had no illusions.

This was it. The end. In a few seconds the sand would close overhead. The hordes of Contams would tear him apart before he was even dead. His last sight would be their jaws ripping piece of his arms and legs from his bloodied body. The desert erupted into terminal screams as Phoenix went down. . . .

The Contams were howling in mortal agony

as the flesh was incinerated on their bones. A stream of fire was washing over them, sending them running and spinning like flaming tops as they were roasted alive. Trench couldn't see the source of the flamethrower, but he knew he had a chance.

Whipping his K-BAR from its sheath, Trench sawed the survival knife's serrated blade across one of the hands trying to drag him down to hell.

Blood spurted as the hand fell away from its wrist, still clutching his leg. With all his strength he clawed his way to the top of the sand pit.

"Come on!" yelled the runt with the flame-thrower. Contams were scattering in every direction. Those that were on fire flung them-selves to the hot sand and rolled frantically in their efforts to extinguish the flames. But the napalm jelly adhered to their bodies and they died with agonizing slowness. The survivors would burrow into the desert sand like diseased crabs, to wait for easier prey in the cool of the night.

Trench couldn't help suppress a laugh as he saw the guy with the flamethrower. He was a midget. The midget wore an eye patch over his left eye. Scraggly blond hair hung down under a snap-brimmed Stetson.

The tanks of highly flammable liquid napalm were as large as he was and the huge ejection tube was longer than he was tall. The midget obviously didn't like being laughed at by the much taller man. He glared belligerently up at Trench.

"Something funny, pal?" he asked.

"Sorry," Trench returned. "It's just that I—"

"—just that you find the guy who saved your ass is a midget, right?" The little guy frowned. "Yeah, I guess that's a real stomach-ripper." He

shrugged off the flamethrower rig. "Well, it just
so happens I'm not a midget at all," he said.

"Oh yeah?" Trench asked.

"Yeah. I happen to be the world's smallest
giant." Trench looked down at the midget. The
midget looked up at Trench. Both broke out
laughing.

"You always carry around a flamethrower or
just on special occasions?" Trench asked.

"This here's a U.S.-Army-issue thrower,"
returned the little man. "Found it. Figured I'd
sell it to a dude I know in Vegas."

Trench introduced himself and the midget
said his name was Big Wally. When Trench again
stopped laughing, the midget explained that he'd
been out in the desert prospecting with a metal
detector for junk he could sell in Trinity when
he'd seen the chase.

"I figured anybody those clowns from
Trinity hated so much to chase after was an all
right guy," Big Wally said as they got into his
truck, a beat-up Ford pickup parked around a
nearby dune. The bed of the truck was piled with
articles of every description. There were bottles,
machinery, plumbing fixtures, and just plain
junk. Mostly there were odds and ends scavenged
from the wrecks of cars. A sign on the truck's side
said, "Big Wally's Salvage." "What was that all
about anyway, Kemo Sabe?"

"It's a long story," Trench answered.

"Yeah, I'll *bet*," Big Wally said. "Where you
want me to drop you, Kemo Sabe?" he asked after
a span of silence. "I'm heading into Vegas myself.
Believe me, you don't want to be out on this
highway after nightfall. The Contams are as thick
as night crawlers after a heavy rain. Used to be
this here stretch of Interstate was the main route
between Vegas and L.A. The Contams, I guess,

were once truckers, townspeople, who knows
what."

Trench told him Vegas was as good a place as
any. He needed wheels now, as well as ammo.
Chances were good he'd find some there.

Big Wally kept eyeballing Trench. "You
weren't in Frisco recently, were you, pal?" he
asked. "We been getting reports of some heavy
goings-on there. Some Lone Ranger dude did a
solo nuke job on the Presidio SCORF base. Some
guy with a tattoo..." Big Wally's voice trailed
off as he saw the Phung Hoang above Trench's
heart. "Like the one . . . you . . ."

"Well fuck a duck," he soon said softly. Big
Wally shoved a tape cassette into the pickup's
player. The cab filled with Procol Harem's
"Whiter Shade of Pale."

4

Big Wally's beat-up Ford pickup rolled crankily down the highway, passing the rusting wrecks of junked cars and trucks K.O.ed when electro-magnetic pulses from the nuclear airbursts had blown their ignition systems months before. The hulks still littered the landscape.

World War III had given new meaning to the word blitzkreig. It had been over sooner than it took to digest a pizza. Since Vegas was closer to Los Angeles than it was to its nearest neighbor in Nevada, Reno, State Route 15 had always been a fast route for Angelinos to take to the hot and fast action next door.

But when the nukes had hit, Route 15 had become a very narrow escape corridor for millions of people running wildly from the blazing inferno L.A. had become. The blacktop corridor to a safe haven had also become the world's biggest obstacle course. Heavily armed badass heist crews had dogged the refugee caravans, ripping off the escaping Angelinos and leaving them without wheels. The Contams had finished off most before they could even reach Vegas. The road had ended up as the world's longest grave-yard.

The city of Las Vegas, although trashed by the nukes that took it out along with the silos of the Nellis Air Force Range and Nuclear Test Site nearby, was still everything it once had been, only in a different way.

From a distance of two miles out in the desert, you could still make out the charred steel exoskeleton of the once-glittering tower of the Landmark Hotel and Casino. The neon-lit Casino Center on southern Las Vegas Boulevard was now a mass of twisted steel structures, firestorms having blackened the denuded girders of its hotels.

"Checkpoint," Big Wally told Phoenix. The pickup braked to a halt before a barricade of trashed autos and concrete-block vehicle traps. Badassed dudes wielding automatic shotguns and assault rifles manned the barricades. But they didn't seem bent on trouble. One of them took a cursory look inside Big Wally's cab and waved them on. It was obvious that he was a familiar sight to the sentries. The other handed Trench a yellow handbill. It read:

PROCLAMATION

You are entering Las Vegas under the protection of Sheik Abdullah X. Shabazz the First.

You are permitted to carry weapons, but they must be surrendered at the order of the Sheik's representatives.

Entry of Contams into the city of Las Vegas is strictly prohibited. The penalty is death by immediate execution for any person caught harboring a Contam.

Have fun and enjoy your visit.

"You heard of the Sheik?" Big Wally asked Phoenix.

Trench shook his head.

"The Sheik of Las Vegas," Big Wally went on. "The town was drowning in its own blood until he moved in and made peace. The Mafia and the biker gangs were snuffing each other for control of the casinos' action.

"People still need the kind of stuff Vegas offers. The gambling, the pussy, the high rolling, the night life. Nowadays, the Sheik gets a piece of everything that goes down in Vegas. He sees all, he hears all. You fart in the wrong key, the Sheik knows about it before you even smell it."

It was the freak show at the end of the world.

Running west by southwest and intersecting with Fremont Street at its apex, Las Vegas Boulevard formed a six-mile triangle with the downtown Casino Center inside it.

What the locals had renamed "the Bermuda Triangle" was now lined with the almost intact and partially destroyed wreckage of the luxury hotels and world-class casinos that had once bathed it nightly in a technicolor sea of scintillating neon.

Most of these establishments were still open for business. Traffic was heavy up and down the Strip and the pavements were thronged with action-seekers. As in pre-N-Day Vegas, most had ridden in and would ride out again. Unlike most of Vegas's former visitors, these tourists in hell carried heavy artillery instead of credit cards and gambled with their lives.

The majority of the cruisers on the Strip were badasses. Stoked on drugs they and their women or whores for the night formed a moving wall of leather, metal, and ultra-bad vibes.

They were the predators of post-nuke America, sporting the regalia of the fierce New Order. Chains, spikes, heavy metal, heavy leather. They had come from all around to party. And to them, no party was a success unless somebody turned belly-up and died.

As night fell, the temperature dropped 20 degrees in as many minutes. A lemon-drop moon hung in a pitch-black sky.

Big Wally, his little legs struggling to keep pace with Phoenix as they shouldered through the nighttime freak world on the Strip, realized that the crowds were heavier than usual because of the Murder Marathon.

As part of the Sh'ek's peacekeeping arrangement, a motorized tournament was to be held in which wheelmen representing Vegas and its rival cities and towns would duel to the death in fast cars equipped with heavy weapons.

The winning driver would earn his people tribute from their neighbors.

The whores and the merchants of every sort of commodity were doing a rack-up business due to the mammoth crowds attracted by the upcoming Murder Marathon. Prostitutes openly displayed their wares, often performing sex with their johns out in the open. The bed of a pickup was as good as any other bed, and doing the dirty deed standing up was as good as doing it lying down.

"You know where I can score some weapons and ammo?" Phoenix asked Big Wally.

The midget said he did. "But you want a beer first, right? Then you want to get fucked, I bet. Well, pardnuh, I know this woman, she's got such a fine—"

"Wrong," Trench said cutting Big Wally off. "Iron first, beer later, pussy last."

"Can I quote you on that, big guy?" Big Wally asked, shaking his head. "I mean, no shit, people must tell you all the time you're a regular fount of wisdom, right?"

They made their way through the garish crowds, past neon-lit dens where gunshots and shrieks could be heard above the cacophony of mindlessly driving, pounding, pulsing music. Midway along the main drag, they rounded a corner, followed an ill-lit series of back streets, and approached a door. Big Wally knocked three times long, three times short.

"Bewitched, bewitched, you've got me in your spell," a voice sang out.

"Bewitched, bewitched, I know that voice so well," the midget returned. "Brought you a customer, Thunderdog."

A squat dude with a badly burned face led them down into the basement, locking the steel firedoor behind him. The basement was an arsenal. Racks on its walls were crammed with small arms of every description.

A firing range lit by overhead fluorescents ran the length of a narrow corridor. Backed by sandbags, bullseyes and cutout targets were ready.

"This is Thunderdog," Big Wally said to Trench. "He owes me, don't you, Thunderdog?" The man dourly shook his head. He obviously did owe Big Wally, because he didn't seem like the sort of guy to give anything freely.

Thunderdog sullenly produced a factory-fresh MINIMI somewhat smaller than the light machine gun Trench had lost in the Contam ambush. It was the carbine version of the lethal M249. "Try her out," the weaponeer said. Trench grabbed iron and pointed at one of the bullseyes at the other end of the range. The MINIMI belched. The target disintegrated.

Trench explained his munitions needs and was outfitted with several hundred rounds of ammo for the MINIMI and his two empty Micro Uzis, several grenades—including cartridges for his HK grenade-launching pistol, and fresh Hush Puppy silencers.

"Where to now, Phoenix?" asked Big Wally as they left. "Check out the nightlife? Maybe you want a girl?"

Trench regarded the cigar-chomping midget. "Why don't you get lost?" he said. "I'm grateful for your help and I mean no offense, but you're beginning to give me heartburn, little man."

"Hey, I saved your life, remember?" said the midget, gesturing with his cigar. "That means you owe me one, Kemo Sabe. And don't you fucking forget it. I'm sticking with you until I get me a chance to collect on your debt."

Phoenix turned and stalked away. The little man followed, huffing and puffing with exertion.

"Hey, goddamnit!" he yelled. "Wait up!"

Bubbles Bixby kneaded her huge breasts as she prepared herself for the night's work. She had always enjoyed sex and so using her cunt to trade for her life was not much of a problem. Except for the glitter, it wasn't that different from show biz.

Not too long ago, Bubbles had been one of Vegas's highest-paid lounge performers, pulling down three hundred large ones a night. Then her career had started to turn brown around the edges and she had become a professional girl-friend to a succession of Mafia kingpins to keep body and soul together. Now the only way to make it in Vegas was by playing the Sheik's game.

Vince Sators, a.k.a. "The Sheik of Las

Vegas" and "Abdullah X. Shabazz," came in from the purple-tiled bathroom. He was nude, ready for sex. Bubbles came over and took him into her mouth. She sucked him deep and he fondled her huge breasts, tweaking the long nipples so hard she screamed.

"Yeah!" he grunted. "Suck it, bitch!"

Bubbles scarfed pecker with a vengeance. Finally getting enough, the Sheik got down between her legs. It smelled good. He nuzzled her, rutting around in the satiny wetness of her cooze. Then he threw her legs over his massive shoulders and sank in his bulldozing tool.

Bubbles moaned and pumped against him. "Oh God!" she shrieked, urging him on. "Do me harder!"

The Sheik thrust faster and deeper, going into his short strokes as orgasm almost arrived. When it finally did, he came with a loud animal grunt, throwing back his head as he filled the slut with his hot, spurting seed.

A hidden camera captured all of the Sheik's sexual prowess for later viewing. Later, he'd screen the woman's performance. If she passed muster, he'd include her in his harem. If she didn't, well . . . there were always plenty of buyers for second-quality pussy.

The Sheik was still deciding whether to give the latest applicant a second try when his private phone rang. Whacking her on the ass, he got up to go to it, lighting up a long joint of quality grass from the underground tanks he ran as part of the Vegas operation.

Thanks to his hydroponic pot garden, Vegas grass was second only to the weed that came from Earthwomb, a freak religious cult out in the desert. He didn't know what their secret was, but for the Sheik it was fertilizer: ground-up humans, he'd found, made the plants grow the best.

On the line was the Sheik's Grand Vizier, Emilio "the Spider" Tarantola. Before the Sheik had taken over, the Spider had been capo of the most powerful Mafia family in Las Vegas, raking in millions in illegal skim operations and controlling all the major rackets in Sin City.

But cut off from the Godfathers back East, Emilio had realized that his only chance of surviving the scramble for power in post-nuke Vegas lay in throwing what muscle he had left solidly behind the Sheik. The remnants of the former capo's crew of vicious buttonmen now formed the nucleus of the Sheik's Royal Guardsmen, while the mob honcho himself was now the cat's-paw of the man who had once taken orders from him.

"What is it?" asked the Sheik. "It better be good. I got some prime cunt here tonight, man." He looked over at the bimbo. Bubbles blew the Sheik a kiss.

Emilio sat in the mobile phone hooked into the dashboard of his Grand Vizier's royal stretch limo. He surveyed the scene of a barroom brawl. The corpse was going to prove very dangerous for the Spider. He would have to watch how he relayed the news.

"We got a problem, Chief," Emilio said. "Cadillac Jack's been whacked."

"What is this, some kind of a jawbeaker?" returned the Sheik. "As in saying, 'Cadillac Jack's been whacked,' three times fast? Am I supposed to think this is funny or something, Emilio?"

"This ain't no joke, Chief."

The Sheik was silent. He was silent only when he was mad. Cadillac Jack was the driver who was to represent Vegas in the Murder Marathon. The Murder Marathon was three days away. Jack was good. He was the tri-state driving champ and had taken out the best the opposition could offer. He left bodies piled in his slipstream. Nobody had anybody as good as him.

"Find me a replacement," the Sheik said. His voice was calm, betraying the anger boiling up inside him. Emilio sensed this.

"But Chief—"

"No buts about it," the Sheik returned, his voice now reflecting the strain of keeping his emotions on a tight rein. "You find that man or you are one dead hombre. And another thing, Emilio . . ."

"What's that, Chief?"

The Sheik paused for a long beat. "*Don't ever call me Chief, you dumb asshole,*" he said and hung up hard.

Emilio heard the click as the receiver was racked at the other end. He motioned to his underlings to carry the body away, then told them to stop. He pulled back the sheet covering Cadillac Jack's face.

"You fuckin' hump!" he cursed. A gob of spit flew into the corpse's face. "He goes into the grass tanks. He turns into a joint. May he burn in hell."

In his room atop the former Caesar's Palace Hotel on the corner of Stardust and Convention Center Drive, the Sheik of Las Vegas strode to the window. He looked down at the neon madness of the lights below, the neon he'd brought back from where there'd been only ashes.

Beyond, to the north and southeast, smaller, dimmer fairy-shimmers of lights marked the locations of the towns of Trinity, Devil's Pitchfork, Hellhole, Gomorrah, and Crucifixion. They were controlled by badass warlords who itched to send their freak armies on a plundering, killing, and raping junket. But a delicate Pax Las Vegas had been established at the end of the bloody turf wars that marked the months following N-Day.

That peace, the Sheik knew, would rely heavily on the Murder Marathon's outcome. It would be more than just a joust on wheels, and its winner would determine more than just which town received the allotments of food, women, money, gasoline, arms, and other precious commodities that were paid to the victor's camp. It would also be a subtle test of strength that put on display the might of every participant. The Murder Marathon would take the place of the open turf wars, establishing the pecking order among the five cities in the region, each of which would send its finest wheelman to compete in the motorized death duel.

With Cadillac Jack, the Sheik had been satisfied that fear would be struck into the opposition's heart. Jack would have trashed his adversaries. He was the best demolition man on wheels. Nobody could come up against him and live. It could be suicide if Vegas ever looked like a wimp city in front of the opposition. His town had it good and was a lot softer than it let on. The Sheik knew there was a fine line between looking like a wimp and getting treated like one.

That asshole Emilio's job had been to keep a tight rein on Cadillac Jack. Nobody was allowed to get within spitting distance of him without being put through a security sieve. The Sheik knew that hired assassins, either free-lance or contract, would look good taking out Vegas's best Wheelman before the Murder Marathon. And now some kill-crazy punk had done just that. The Sheik was mad enough to spit. His cock stood up, purple in anger, banging against his stomach.

"Ooooh, I'm still horny," Bubbles cooed on the bed. He could smell her cooze from across the room. It gave off a deep, musky aroma. Combined with the effects of the marijuana, it was driving him crazy.

He crossed to the bed and pinned her down. Crouching on her chest, he rammed his huge phallus into her mouth. She took it all into her throat, gagging on the nine-inch choker. He pumped it between her tits and came his load all over her face.

Satisfied, the Sheik watched while she licked it off.

This broad was strictly second-rate. The Sheik made a mental note to sell her as soon as possible to the scuzz from Devil's Pitchfork. She was just their speed. He also made himself a mental note to get himself a new second in command. Tarantola had fucked up one last time.

"Get your MAC 10 blazin', snuff a dozen people. . . ." The lyrics to the Mad Mutants' "Born to Be Dead" blared over the megawatt public-address system in the smoke-filled Pioneer Casino." *"Lookin' for some bodies and a flame-thrower to burn 'em . . ."*

Hardcase punks in black leather, aluminum-spike Mohawks, and chrome chains mingled with a more sedate crowd with furs and jewelry covering their radiation burns. Both groups bristled with guns.

The crowd could have been pre-nuke, except for a few changes that went beyond the fact that the furs were fake, the jewelry glass, and the casinos housed in the charred skeletons of steel girders draped with canvas for walls.

In the first place, the security staff no longer kept a low profile. Tough dudes armed with heavy metal walked loud and carried heavy firepower.

The usual games, such as blackjack, keno, roulette, and craps, were still around, but there were some new additions to keep up with the savage tempo of savage times.

Blitzkrieg, Deathtrap, Kneecap, and Meat-grinder were three of the most popular.

In addition to cigarette girls, house cock-suckers went around giving free fluff jobs. You could play blackjack and get your prick licked at the same time.

"Nice gun," cooed a casino cocksucker, stroking the barrel of Trench's MINIMI. "So big and so long. Wanna shoot a few wet ones into my pussy?" Her hand traveled to Trench's crotch. "You can do me on a blackjack table or in one of the rooms upstairs. Upstairs costs, though." He brushed away the bimbo's hand as Big Wally hustled toward the action.

A game of Meatgrinder—a form of Russian Roulette in which SMGs were used instead of more familiar revolvers—was about to begin. Two zombie scavs in leather and spikes sat across from each other at a table while the referee called for betters to lay their money down.

"Watch the dude with the safety pin through his nose," Big Wally told Trench after he'd placed his bet with the referee. "He's got icewater running through his veins."

The referee held a pair of MAC 10 subguns over his head and shoved in two clips, then laid the MACs between the two Meatgrinder players. Keeping his hands on the SMGs, the ref circled the weapons around a few times to show the spectators there was no chance of his having rigged the contest—running a clean game was essential to the referee's staying alive long enough to show a profit.

Locking his eyes on his opponent, Safety-Pin Scav picked up the MAC that lay in front of him and, with a perverted smile on his pale white features, jammed the machine pistol's muzzle into his mouth. At the same time, his opponent—a leather badass with a cueball skull and a mass of Plague blisters for the right half of his face—grabbed heavy metal and jammed his MAC's business-end up against the deformed mass of abscessed head growths.

Safety-Pin Scav screamed as he squeezed the MAC's trigger. The bolt jumped forward but snapped on an empty firing chamber with a loud metallic sound. He laid the MAC back down in front of him and folded his arms. Cueball Head jerked his weapon's trigger but wasn't as lucky as his opposition.

Blowback made ugly yellow flame spurt from the SMG's breech as a trio of spent shell casings flew out the ejector port. The full-auto quickburst blew a fist-sized entry wound in Cueball Head's skull as the entire right half of the geek's face exploded outward in a miniature red supernova of jet-propelled bone, blood, and brain matter. Momentum in the direction of the blast knocked the faceless corpse over on its chair, fountaining crimson from the severed arterial tubes in the jagged neck stump.

The referee held up Safety-Pin Sav's hand and declared him winner and still champion. Then, after Cueball Head was carried to the dumpsters out back, to be piled with the night's other loses at Meatgrinder, another opponent sat down to try his luck against the undefeated Safety-Pin Scav.

"Always bet on the favorite," the midget said as he counted his winnings. "That's the secret of success."

* * *

Big Wally directed Trench toward the concierge's desk.

"You want pussy?" the concierge asked. "Beautiful girls. Clean. No radiation. Some of these cheap bimbos you find at the Sevens or the Palace—no offense to the Sheik—they die sucking your cock. No kidding, they get lockjaw around your shank and sometimes they bite it right off. Now, our girls are the finest. Like you never—"

Trench pulled the concierge across the desk.

"Just a room," he said.

"Yessir!" returned the concierge. "Like I was saying, just a room." He handed them a key. "Now you're gonna want some smoke, some crack, some SPASM. . . ."

Cockroaches as big as squirrels crawled over the walls. Chirping cockroaches. But at least the room had a view—that is, if you liked twisted girders. Despite everything, Trench was sound asleep in seconds. It had been a long, hard day in nuclear hell.

5

The Cobra gunship hovered over the LZ, a bull-dozed strip in downtown Chicago containing inflatable building modules which the map identified as Garfield Park but which was now just another nuclear moonscape like everything else. The armed-to-the-teeth attack copter lurched as it descended and came to rest on its skids, kicking up a cloud of dust.

John Tallon, wearing NBC-resistant Saratoga combat fatigues in a standard NATO camo pattern, jumped from the chopper's cockpit. The SCORF honcho pulled the collar of his battle jacket up against a wind so cold it burned his skin as it howled across the South Shore from the frozen surface of Lake Michigan.

"I'll radio when I want to return," he told the chopper pilot. The Cobra's turbines screamed as Tallon and two SCORF mercs crossed the LZ, whipping up devils of dust as the copter lifted off and banked in an 80-degree arc, disappearing north to the SCORF hardbase at Skokie.

"How soon can we begin?" Tallon asked the officer who had come to greet him. The officer

wore a uniform with insignia identifying him as
the SCORF NETDZ Regional Commander and
with a name tag, below the left collar, identifying
him as Havelock.

"Immediately, sir," Havelock replied,
saluting briskly. "The fire zone is nearby. My
driver will have us there in a few minutes." The
Commander pointed toward a HUMMER
stationed nearby with an armed escort of two
squat black M706 APCs. Each of the armored,
track-mounted, all-terrain personnel carriers was
manned by a driver and M-60 machine gunner
combo.

A command post had been set up at the top of
a 30-story structural steel stump that had once
been a mammoth skyscraper called the Sears
Tower. It overlooked a cratered, wreckage-strewn
hellzone that had once been the bustling urban
center of Michigan Boulevard.

A lone figure jumped from the top of the fire-
blackened husk of a Chicago Transit Authority
bus onto the torn-up asphalt of the street with
catlike grace. In his hand he clutched a Heckler-
Koch MP38 SMG with a banana clip containing
36 9-mm wadcutter slugs.

"His code name is Bloodstone," the Commander informed Tallon. "I think this exhibition
will demonstrate exactly what you want."

Tallon didn't answer. Why should he, when
the Commander knew damn well that, if it didn't,
he'd peel his balls with a bottle opener? The
SCORF honcho wordlessly snatched up the bino-
culars dangling from his neck and focused them
on the fire zone below.

Three zombie scavs, armed with automatic
rifles, suddenly ran from within the hulking
wreckage of a nuked skyscraper's lobby,

screaming like banshees. Each had been promised resettlement in one of the Radiation Free Zones in the Northwest if they would do what had come naturally to them in the months since the NBC holocaust had hurled them back to the Stone Age: kill one lone man.

The scavs lost no time in starting their attack.

They opened up with autofire. A withering cross-hail of death was focused with the lone commando at its apex.

The bullets spanged off bare brick. The solo had disappeared. With an unbelievable quickness, he darted for the cover of an overturned garbage truck. Lobbing three smoke grenades in quick succession, the merc sprinted through the thick pall of black smoke, reappearing at a three-o'clock angle to the scavs. By the time they reacted, it was all over.

A staccato capture burst of autofire from a HK 9-mm SMG catapulted the scav trio a million years into the future in a flashburst of lethal liberation before they could even bring their weapons into position.

With robot-like precision, the merc commando severed their heads and held the gruesome decapitated trophies overhead in his raised arms, a token of victory.

"Good," Tallon said. "Tell him to report to my office after he's cleaned up."

"I said you would be pleased," the Commando told him.

"It's a good thing for you I am," Tallon said before turning and stalking toward the elevator that had brought him up through the Sears Tower's steel skeleton, "or you'd be building an igloo in Alaska before you could snap your fingers."

**CLASSIFIED: TOP SECRET
OPERATIONAL URGENT**

FR BIG STONE GAP/ENOCH 387Q#5
TO NESTRN REG CMND/TALLON

BT

SUBJECT PHOENIX SIGHTED X TRACKED
BY SCORF SOG GROUP DIVISION COM-
MAND LOWER FRESNO AREA X HAS
BEEN HIGHLY MOBILE SINCE LEAVING
SF AND DESTROYING SCORF HARDBASE
WITH NUKE EXPLOSIVE X FROM FRESNO
HAS AVOIDED SCORF PATROLS AND
BRIEFLY DISAPPEARED FROM SUR-
VEILLANCE FOR APPROX NINETY DAYS
WITHOUT ANY SIGN OF SUBJECT
REPORTED BY FIELD OPERATIVES X
SUBJECT RESURFACED ON INTERSTATE
HGHWY RT 95 WHEN SIGHTED BY
RESCUE PERSONNEL ENGAGED IN
CONTAM EXTERMINATION IN WSTRN
NEVADA X PHOENIX SIGHTED BY SOG
OPS ENTERING TOWN OF TRINITY
NEVADA ON MORNING OF 23RD X
IMMUNE BOUNTY HUNTERS ALSO
SIGHTED TARGET USING CAM SUB-
STANCE SNIFFER AND WERE OBSERVED
FOLLOWING PHOENIX INTO TRINITY
WITH OBJECT OF APPREHENSION TO
COLLECT STANDING BOUNTY X VIOLENT
CONFRONTATION RESULTING IN
PITCHED FIREFIGHT ENSUED X
SUBJECT ESCAPED IN STOLEN 4 X 4 AND
WAS GIVEN CHASE BY REMNANTS OF
TRINITY'S SURVIVING POPULATION X
PITCHED BATTLE ENSUED IN WHICH
TARGET SINGLEHANDEDLY KILLED AT
LEAST FIFTY PURSUERS AND DES-
TROYED SIXTY VEHICLES OF VARYING

TYPES X SUBJECT CURRENT IN CITY OF
LAS VEGAS NEVADA X PLEASE ADVISE
ON STATUS OF TARGET PHOENIX X

ACKNOWLEDGE AND CONFIRM

BT
9870#2
EOM

Tallon crumpled the telex and flung it to the
floor. He would order surveillance on the god-
forsaken Phung Hoang until he gave the order
otherwise.

With Bloodstone, the final member of the
assassination squad, in place, his operation code-
named Pact of Steel was nearly ready. In the
coming weeks, grueling military training would
whip these already skilled combatants into a
lethal force of full-auto fastgunners who would
search out and destroy the Alpha-Immune and
end his threat to the New Order once and for all.

For the present, Magnus Trench would be
allowed to wallow in the illusion that his life was
his own, like a pig in a mudbath being fattened for
the slaughter.

But that illusion would crumble to dust when
the merc crew he'd assembled was ready. It
would come down on the Phoenix guy like a
thousand tons of trouble. And he would be
obliterated beneath its onrushing weight like an
ant in the path of a bulldozer.

Tallon wrote out a response to the telex and
handed it to an aide for coded transmission to
Enoch at his Big Stone Gap, Virginia, head-
quarters. Buried three miles beneath the earth in
his high-tech bunker like some freakish mole-
man, Enoch had become obsessed with one thing:
becoming a man again.

If not for the best medical technology available, the Dark Messiah would have long since slipped into a Contam state. But the biosurvival suit that encased his diseased body in a steel cocoon was a prison for his mind as well.

On the verge of psychosis, Enoch needed the Alpha-Immune's Plague antibodies for an emergency bone-marrow implant to restore his mutating organs to normalcy after contracting the Contam Plague. The deadly Russian supervirus had penetrated even the supposedly fail-safe-activated charcoal NBC filters in his bunker's multimillion-dollar ventilation system.

And Tallon would see that the Dark Messiah received that life-giving bone-marrow implant. He would also personally supervise the death of the man who had made him look like a bozo, the man who had used one of Tallon's own miniature nuclear bombs to blast his Presidio SCORF base in north San Francisco to radioactive embers.

Tallon would see to it that Phoenix's death would be as slow as it was agonizing and a hundred times more humiliating.

The merc honcho relished the technicolor fantasy-image of Trench pleading for the end, begging him to put him out of his misery. He imagined himself a hundred feet tall and Trench a pygmy, holding Phoenix cupped in the palm of his hand like a vengeful colossus before crushing him to pulp.

The thought reminded Tallon that some scav troublemakers were going to be executed soon. The merc smiled, looking forward to seeing them offed. He hoped he'd have time for a little lunch first.

The SCORF training facility in the Northwestern Uncontaminated Zone (UZ)—an area of

virtually unspoiled timberland protected from
ionizing radiation by a huge geodesic dome
encased in a plexiglass bubble—had been selected
both for its short distance by air from the target
area and for its round-the-clock maximum
security provided by a garrison of troops.

The Blue Mountains of the Pacific Northwest
had been one of the few regions of the North
American continent that had been relatively undamaged by nuclear blast and uncontaminated
by nuclear-charged particles, germ agents,
airborne toxins, and gas-dispersed chemical
poisons released into the ecosystem.

Accustomed to the oppressively brutal
environments of the hellzones in which they had
seen action, the mercs Tallon had handpicked for
his assault team were at first disoriented in their
new, pre-nuke surroundings.

But the psychs had warned him to expect the
mercs to freak out at the shock of sensory overload on nervous systems accustomed to chronic
sensory deprivation. Seeing nature as it had once
existed, and as it wouldn't exist again over much
of the world for several centuries, might in fact
drive some completely over the edge of insanity.

The psychs had also warned Tallon that the
sensory overload might blunt the savage
brutality he had chosen the mercs for. Sadism,
they explained, was largely a response to the
sensory deprivation produced by life in the bleak
environment of nuked cities. Brutality and sex
were the only ways of generating the much-
needed sensory input. Without this warped
pursuit of violence, their minds might atrophy.
Perversion was their antidote to a world gone
mad.

Tallon had personally developed a saturation
course in tactical military deployment which was

geared to maximizing the fighting efficiency of the warriors he had brought to the UZ facility. Weapons courses where death awaited those who were too slow or not hard enough to fire at live targets brought home the reality of what the mercs were to experience.

Tallon faced the men and took stock of them.

The merc with the code name Fast Dancer, the best of the group, was a lockjawed simian with glittering gray eyes. He was a veteran of SCORF operations in the Central TDZ and of refugee-control operations at the liquidation center for dangerous exiles at St. Louis, Missouri.

Deathlock was shorter but muscular and cunning. He had been the only surviving member of a garrison in Alaska that had skirmished with a Russkie invasion force.

Saggitar, an NCSC recruit from the Eastern Seaboard, was anxious to gain acceptance into the higher echelons of SCORF; Tallon was somewhat reluctant but Saggitar had proven his value in silent and efficient contract hits ordered by the merc honcho himself.

Moebius was an old hand at killing efficiently and silently. The merc had been formerly assigned to the San Francisco hardbase and had firsthand knowledge of Phoenix's capabilities.

Quicksilver was another SCORF hardguy who had worked in forced organ-transplant operations in the Frisco TDZ. He and Moebius worked effectively together and could effectively double-team the Phung Hoang.

Bloodstone was last. He was a loner from the Chicago Deathlands. He would enjoy killing for its own sake. They all did there.

The primary training-response data and psychology workups on each man were encouraging. But not good enough. If they were to be ready soon enough to do Tallon any good, the team would have to be raised to a fever pitch.

"Around you," Tallon barked, "has been constructed a maze of booby traps. You are to navigate this obstacle course and come out not only alive, but completely unharmed. If any man is injured, he will be sent back to his place of origin. I don't want any losers on this mission. I only want winners. Understood?"

"Yes!" came their answer in resounding unison. "Sir!"

"Good," Tallon called back.

The course was the most grueling his sadistic and devious mind could devise. It incorporated computerized firing devices and live targets, mostly scavs hungry and anxious to kill to earn better treatment. Tallon expected no casualties. The reports on each of his mercs told him that they were survivors to the last man.

"Go!" he barked and watched his windup supermercs scramble for their lives against odds calculated to kill ordinary men in just under 80 seconds. But they weren't ordinary men. You could tell because they seemed to love it.

CLASSIFIED: TOP SECRET
OPERATIONAL URGENT

FR NESTRN REG CMND/TALLON
TO BIG STONE GAP/ENOCH 387Q#6

SPECIAL STRIKE FORCE TRAINING PROCEEDING X PHOENIX SIGHTING ACKNOWLEDGED AND UNDERSTOOD X DO NOT REPEAT DO NOT ATTEMPT TO APPREHEND TARGET UNTIL FURTHER INSTRUCTIONS RECEIVED X INDICATIONS ARE TARGET WILL REMAIN STATIONARY FOR SOME TIME X STRIKE FORCE TRAINING WILL

COINCIDE WITH CONCERTED ATTACK ON
SUBJECT X THIS TIME THERE WILL BE NO
FAILURES

ACKNOWLEDGE AND CONFIRM

TB
9870#2
EOM

6

The Circus Maximus of Caesar's Palace was now a lot closer to its namesake than the big-bucks investors who had erected it had originally intended.

The ring formed the focal point of the circular tiers of seats comprising the bowl of the vast indoor arena. Heavyweight championship prize-fights had been held here, including the Ali-Spinks bout in 1982. These days, the stakes were a lot higher than even a multimillion-dollar purse, and far simpler.

The stakes were life and death.

You just didn't get any higher or simpler.

Cinderblock corridors beyond the arena had been converted into gladiatorial pens where those condemned to die in the arena were kept before the mortal combat began.

Since the crimes for which a man might be sentenced to death in Vegas were as common as snot on a hankie, there was no shortage of talent for the ring. The combatants here were the ultimate throwaways in a throwaway world.

With ringside seats, Phoenix and Big Wally

had a close-up of the end of the second warmup bout before the main gladiatorial event started. The bout featured two women who had flailed away at each other for a full 20 minutes, first with crude clubs bristling with spikes, then with mailed fists, teeth, and anything else they could use as weapons.

The defender, a Hopi Indian calling herself Mad Maxine, was up against the champion, a tall blonde called Piltdown Annie. Dressed in a buckskin costume, Mad Maxine warily circled her opponent. In one gauntleted hand, she brandished a steel-headed tomahawk.

Annie was wearing chain mail and wicked spikes on her wrists, elbows, and kneecaps. The spiked head of Annie's mace dangled from a heavy chain as each feinted and tried to psyche the other out.

At first it had looked like the contender might have a chance, but Annie had quickly disarmed Mad Maxine with a body feint to the right and an overhand swipe with the mace that had crippled her right hand. Now, after quickly dealing her opponent a series of crippling body blows, Annie was moving in for the coup de grace.

The capacity audience roared with approval as Mad Maxine kicked out in a last-ditch attempt to knock her opponent off balance. The strategy wound up costing her heavily. As Mad Maxine whipped a bowie knife from her boot and lunged for Annie's heart, Annie scored a fast takedown which knocked Maxine to the canvas. Maxine's breasts showed clearly through her torn shirt. They were covered with scratches and her fat nipples were erect on their heaving mounds.

"Smoke the bitch!" yelled a dude with an eye patch, hefting a bottle of beer.

"Hey, fuck you!" a Mohawk-sporting badass

in black leather from down the aisle challenged, his horse's tail shaking as he angrily shook his fist. "I got fifty riding on her."

Eye Patch settled the argument by whipping out a 9-mm Viking SMG and opening up with a full-auto blitzkrieg that blew the top of Pony Tail's head into the bleachers. Spectators in the corpse's immediate vicinity dove for cover to avoid the lead firestorm, getting spattered with gore as the corpse pitched spastically forward and fell twitching and jerking into the arena's lower tiers.

Pony Tail's mangled corpse was quickly forgotten as Piltdown strapped on a 14-inch, chrome-plated steel dildo to ensure her opponent's final humiliation. The audience cheered wildly as she obscenely gyrated her hips, making the steel phallus glint beneath the hot kliegs. With her slender build, she resembled some androgynous being, neither male nor female.

Tearing the rags from the loser's body, she bullied her into a squatting doggie position.

The crowd cheered wildly as Piltdown forced the huge dildo in and out of Maxine's cunt, then moved to insert the huge steel phallus into the rectum of her vanquished opponent.

An overhead microphone picked up the loser's moans of passion as her breathing quickened and she clawed the canvas in the heat of orgasm. This was Piltdown's trademark. The crowd waited, dead silent, knowing what would happen next.

As Maxine's moans reached their peak intensity, Piltdown pressed a concealed stud on the steel phallus, near the fastenings from which it hung.

Blam! Blam! Blam!

Maxine's urogenital system geysered from the spectacular exit wound in her upper back as the three-round burst of .45 ACP slugs ripped from the muzzle of the steel phallus jutting obscenely from Piltdown's belt.

Piltdown let her opponent's body sag to the canvas. She turned and squatted in front of her. Miraculously, Maxine was still alive. Piltdown pointed her metal penis at Maxine's head, looking at the audience.

A sea of downward-pointing thumbs told her what they wanted. And Piltdown always gave her adoring public *exactly* what they wanted.

A three-round .45-caliber burst coughed from the phallus in a fiery belch.

Maxine's head shattered like a cantaloupe as the explosion blew it into a thousand fragments. Gouts of blood spurted from the jagged neck stump as the corpse collapsed onto its side and began kicking its legs in the air like a headless frog galvanized by an electric current. Blood and brains dripped from the gleaming chrome cock strapped to Piltdown Annie's hips.

Piltdown stood and held her hands high overhead in victory as the audience roared its approval.

Magnus Trench was sickened.

Death was not a sport, although mankind had in its infinite perversity made it just that on countless occasions. The deathsport had taken many forms through the ages. The Roman Empire had called the sport gladiatorial combat. The Middle Ages staged jousts in which the violence and brutality were masked by a chivalrous veneer. In the flexing of chemonuclear muscle that had consumed East and West in the apocalypse of World War III, the deathsport had reached the apex of its barbaric evolution.

Big Wally, sitting beside him, seemed to be wholly in tune with the crowd's violent mood. Guzzling from a jug of Mule Kick shine which he'd bought from a vendor, the little man was cheering as loud as everyone else, high on his own adrenalin.

"She's something, ain't she?" he said to Trench, elbowing him in the ribs. "Puts on some kinda show, rig.it?" He belched loudly, from the shine and dogfurters.

Trench was silent. The runt had the connections he needed to get supplies in this town. He'd stick out the show, but not for much longer.

"You'll get off on the next match, Kemo Sabe," the midget yelled above the crowd's roar. "Guaranteed. Here, have some Mule Kick!" He handed the jug to Trench. Trench broke the jug over the head of a badass sitting behind him who he saw was about to plunge a dagger into his neck. The badass was thrown over the side by the goons sitting around him.

Three cracks of the referee's pistol announced the opening of the next match.

The crowd cheered the favorite, Og Magog, who was a humongous mass of flesh, hair, and muscle with a bullet head. Og Magog came out armed with nothing but his bare hands.

He picked up ringside spectators who'd booed him and banged their heads together until blood seeped from the cracked gourds. He beat a tattoo on his chest while snorting and screaming for the referee to bring on his victims. He looked like he had about as much brains as a box of rocks.

Three badasses only slightly less fearsome-looking than Magog jumped into the ring. They were armed with an assortment of swords, bats, maces, and poleaxes.

Magog made short work of his pug-ugly play-mates, throwing them around like empty garbage cans in a high wind. Without even breaking a sweat, the goliath in the squared circle cleaned house, reducing his crib cousins to mangled corpses.

Going through the theatrical motions of a victory dance, Magog called out for more pushovers from the audience with heavy death-wishes.

"Who wants to raise some hell?" he bellowed. "Five thousand newbucks to the man that kicks my ass!" Newbucks—also called nukebucks—were U.S. dollars devalued at 20 percent of their face value due to the collapse of the money supply after the war.

The audience was silent. As many times as they added up the figures, the total always came out zero. Nobody was megachump enough to believe they had a snowball's chance on a hot griddle of taking Magog out, because it meant the same as killing him. And nobody was under the illusion they could pull that off.

Magog laughed contemptuously and began to say something. "I knew it. You're chickenshit. You're all chi—"

"*My guy will!*"

The midget leaped onto Trench's shoulders. Big Wally shook his little fist and chomped on his stogie. "He'll kick your ass from here to Stalingrad, Magog!"

"Just what the hell do you think you're doing?" asked Trench. He didn't want any part of Magog or the arena. Money wasn't any reason to put your life on the line with some Stone-Age-throwback maniac in the ring.

"You owe me, Kemo Sabe," Big Wally

whispered to Trench. "I saved your nuts, right?
Now the bill comes due."

Whether or not he agreed with Big Wally's
logic, Trench had little choice. The eyes of every
member of the audience were on him. Big Wally
had put him on the spot. He'd either fight Magog or
take on the whole audience. Either way, Trench
would have to fight his way out of the Circus
Maximus. Trench made a mental note to break
the midget's arms and legs if he survived the
bout. Twice.

Big Wally took Trench's weapons, including
his K-BAR survival knife, as Magog watched the
challenger strip off his gear. Seeing Phoenix,
Magog had gone from smug self-confidence to
anxious puzzlement. There was something about
this dude that made him suddenly feel very
uneasy.

Before Trench could climb in, Magog let loose
with a flying body slam that pinned Phoenix
against the ropes. Dazed, he struggled to free
himself as the monster moved in for the kill,
grabbing up a short-handled axe. Holding
Trench's head by the hair, he swung for a vicious
lunge at the windpipe as the audience clamored to
see the victim's head roll into the aisles.

But for Magog, it was like trying to nail jello
to the wall. Trench lashed out with a vicious kick
to Magog's midsection. The giant grunted and
the axe flew from his hands.

Breathing hard and clutching his chest,
Trench squared off against Magog, whose eyes
were now clearly showing the pain. Nobody had
ever hurt him like that. He was going to eat this
turkey alive. It was a matter of honor now.

Magog grabbed Trench in a lethal bear hug.
This was a big mistake. Phoenix head-butted the
giant until he let go. He was dazed but still

dangerous. A series of Choy Li Fut hip thrusts knocked Magog to the canvas.

The crowed roared for Phoenix to finish off Magog. For a brief moment, he glanced away from his prone opponent to face the crowd.

A burst of 9-mm SMG fire reduced Magog to a bullet-riddled corpse. Big Wally stood holding one of Trench's Micro Uzis with its short muzzle smoking.

Trench didn't need to ask why Big Wally had shot Magog when he saw the small derringer his opponent had produced from his high leather boot lying on the canvas an inch from his lifeless hand.

"That's another one you owe me, Kemo Sabe," Big Wally said.

Big Wally was counting his newbucks as he and Trench left the Circus Maximus and made their way down the Vegas Strip.

Trench had decided to grab the nearest set of wheels any way he could and blow town. Vegas wasn't for him. The sooner he hit the highway, the sooner he would be in New York, searching for his wife and son. Not that he had any illusions of his chances of finding them.

Only too well could he see the casualties the war had produced. Its survivors were probably the biggest casualties of all. In the hellworld that was the aftermath of World War III, man had plunged straight through the yawning mouth of hell and crashed to the rock bottom. To the ground floor of creation.

Except for that strangely irrational gut instinct that told him that if Sandra and Brian were dead he would have somehow known, would have somehow flashed telepathically on them, there was no damn reason at all to think they were still alive. And the corporate lawyer Trench had been before again taking up the weapons of death told him never to place his trust in hope, especially blind hope.

In fact, Trench half prayed that his family was no longer alive. They might have been better off that way.

In the six months since N-Day, when he had stood alone on a mountaintop overlooking San Francisco Bay and witnessed the ultimate horror as thermonuclear mushroom clouds engulfed the Bay City in fiery mass annihilation, more than just Planet Earth had sunk into megasavagery.

So had Magnus Trench.

He was no better than the perverted fuckers he so despised. A killing machine, destroying the opposition in the never-ending death struggle that had replaced the comparative order of what he now called the "Pax Americana" with the vacuum of chaos. What were those lofty principles that he thought made him better than the rest when compared with the brutal reality of the lives he took to preserve his own?

Not fucking much, he admitted.

Yeah, maybe the Contam Plague released by Soviet germ-warfare weapons in the USSR's retaliatory strike hadn't infected him.

He was one of the rarest people in America: an Immune, born with antibodies to the TTBP lentivirus that caused wild, mutant growth and submental idiocy in its victims. Hell, he hadn't even suffered so much as minor beta burns from exposure to the nuke blasts, thanks to his quick survival reflexes and a shitload of luck.

But despite this, Trench knew he had been afflicted with a disease nonetheless. It was a disease of the spirit. The disease of violence. And he'd picked up a heavy dose, a madness in his brain and soul which dispensed heavy firepower in the name of justice. But was there any justice strong enough to survive warfare untainted by corruption?

No, there wasn't. Already, he would not have recognized the man he once was. A man with a family, deeply committed to his profession as a corporate lawyer. A man who had argued rationally for justice, not killed for it. A man who had fought his battles with words, not metal. A man who had believed he'd left the Phung Hoang—the Vietnamese Phoenix he'd once been—behind in the steaming jungles of Southeast Asia.

Trench didn't know if his family—even were he by some miracle able to locate them—would even want him back.

"Hey, check out what's happening over there!"

Trench's musings were interrupted by Big Wally's shout. The midget was gesticulating across the Vegas Strip to where a group of men dressed in paramilitary uniforms were trying to drag a young blonde away into a waiting truck. The blonde fought hard, but she wasn't about to do much against the goon squad. A man and a small boy were being held back by other members of the SMG-toting goon squad while the two dudes up front dragged her off, kicking and screaming.

"Yeah, it's Murder Marathon time, all right," Big Wally said with a snicker.

Trench picked the midget up by the buckle of his belt until the little guy's face was at eye level. His little legs bike-pedaled frantically in the air. "Explain," snarled Trench. "Real fast."

"The Sheik's guys . . . they're grabbing the broad for his harem!" Big Wally spluttered, turning beet red as newbucks fluttered to the street frøm his overstuffed pockets. "He always takes his pick, man. He—hey, lemme down! Shit, I'm losing all my money."

Trench dropped the midget, who hit the street with a crash. He scrambled to pick up his scattered newbucks as Trench cocked the bolt of his MINIMI M249, snapping one of Thunderdog's explosive BTHP 9-mm wadcutters into the chamber.

Yeah, Trench thought, when it comes down to the crunch, there was a reason after all.

The best or the worst, depending on what side you were on. *Principle.*

"Hey, man," Big Wally said. "Wuh-what you gonna do?"

Trench smiled. It wasn't at all a pleasant smile.

"Play 'em The Star-Spangled Banner with fifty-pound bombs."

7

Parting like the Red Sea, the milling crowd of
scum-people made way for the showdown they
sensed was about to go critical mass.

In this part of the world, shootouts on main
street were as old as they come. Since the collapse
of American society in the aftermath of nuke
Armageddon, full-auto firefights had become as
common on the streets of Vegas as slaps on the
back had been at other times and other places.

Even the brain-damaged denizens of Nukeworld U.S.A. in their spikes and black leather had
learned to spot the signs of imminent armed
conflict and had the smarts to hightail it away
from ground zero on the double.

Two of the Sheik's Royal Guardsmen in their
modified Afrika Corps action-suits trained 9-mm
parabellum KG/TEC full-auto SMGs on the guy
and the small boy.

What was going down held too many similarities to his own situation for the man called
Phoenix to just let it ride. Some things you could
afford to let ride, but others—no way. Not if you
were any kind of civilized human being. Trench

hoped that if his wife and kid were in the same
situation as these victims, somebody would be
doing what he was about to do.

No, Trench didn't bet on it.

But that didn't matter as far as he was
concerned. You did what you did because every
fiber of your being cried out that it was right, and
you swung with the momentum, unable to ignore
the fire in your belly that screamed at you to take
direct, often violent, action without fear of con-
sequences or expectation of reward.

Trench took out the two badasses holding the
guy and the kid with two pinpoint-accurate
select-fire Uzi heartbursts that revealed the inner
merc as a watermelon-red pulp before the spiffily
attired desert-rat duo could even level the small
but deadly KG/TEC greaseguns into assault
position.

Their two badass pards dragging the kicking,
screaming blonde toward the gaping doors of the
armored personnel-carrier momentarily let the
woman go as they saw the grim-faced avenger
hustle toward them, now packing deadly 7.62-mm
NATO-caliber MINIMI heat.

"Run!" Trench screamed at the woman, who
stood frozen in her tracks as she focused on the
dude charging toward her and the Sheik's
stunned goon squad. As frightening as the two
uniformed royal enforcers might have been, this
guy had them beat by miles.

"Run like hell!" Phoenix repeated, bringing
the lethal MG meatgrinder into position to take
out the two badguys, who were now scrambling
to pull heavy iron out of quick-draw leather. The
blonde finally snapped out of her daze as the guy
with her hustled her and the kid into one of the
casinos fringing the Strip.

The punks in military khakis and high black-

leather boots whipped out ugly black, parkerized
Steyr MPi69 SMGs and dove for cover behind the
olive-drab Jeep four-by-four they'd driven in on
as they emptied 40-round clips of buzzsawing
lead manbusters cycling at 400 rounds per
minute at their agile, mobile, and hostile
adversary.

Deadly whizzers cycloned past Trench's fast-
dodging and hard-to-hit target profile as he
executed a swift tuck-and-roll combination.
Every time the Vegas hit-machines thought
they'd drawn a bead on their target, their
autobursts slammed into an impact zone Phoenix
had occupied only a millisecond before.

Unable to come even close to putting away
the guy who was making jackasses out of the
Sheik of Vegas's elite merc security and
enforcement crew, the Sin City fastgunners gave
no thought to burst control as the ammo supply
of their Steyr SMGs rapidly spewed from the
blazing maws of their impotently spitting
weapons, until the bolts slammed home on empty
chambers.

The Sheik's tissue-paper mercs were about to
learn the hard way what Magnus Trench's friend,
the weapons-master Hamilton Rawlings, had
taught him as the two had hunkered down and
bunkered in at the SCORF merc nest they had
housecleaned after the nuclear apocalypse had
razed Frisco to the ground—that SMG burst
control could mean the difference between life
and death in a full-auto firefight.

Although Rawlings was now a dusting of
ashes scattered on the nuke-blasted lunar surface
of hellhole San Francisco, his teachings had not
been wasted on his pupil Magnus Trench. They
lived on in the mind and combat reflexes of the
man the Dark Messiah's cat's-paws knew and

feared as Phoenix, ready for instant translation into deadly, direct action.

Maybe after the Sheik's rat-prick mercenaries joined Rawlings in the afterlife, the weapons-master would have a chance to drum some sense into their heads in his fast-rapping teaching style. To speed along their meeting, Phoenix was about to arrange a one-way ticket to the spirit world on the wings of a .45 ACP wadcutter firestorm.

In the awkward silence as the Sheik's Royal Guardsmen struggled to snap fresh 40-round mags into the butts of their MPi69 SMGs, Trench cut loose with a screaming MINIMI fusilage of heavy-caliber destruction.

A burst tore into the flesh on the left side of one Steyr gunman's ribcage, sending bone fragments scalpeling through the guy's lungs, heart, and kidneys.

Massive shock trauma flash-boiled the blood in the heart, causing the lungs and pleural cavity to burst open like a water-filled balloon. The gunner started to do a kind of breakdance, kicking out his legs and throwing up his arms in the sitting position.

But the guy's feet never got back under him as he flopped backward and lay still with a dark stain pooling out of his uniform and onto the dusty street.

Hot piss trickled down his pard's pants leg. The merc had never seen death visited so swiftly or grimly on any of the many gun-and-run operations he had participated in throughout his years as a soldier of fortune—even in such stinking hellzones as Namibia or Sri Lanka, or the Third World power struggles that went down with the regularity of Norteamericano flu cases in the banana republics of Central and South America.

The merc returned fire on mental autopilot, managing to reload his Steyr MPi69 SMG in time to cut loose with a high-velocity bullet salvo, using both hands to stabilize the hard-recoiling automatic weapon.

Pulling a sideways double jackknife to present a narrower target profile, Phoenix came out of the fastmove progression in perfect balance. Stabilized on one knee, he fired from the hip as the last of the tinhorn Indians got off a final, wild, three-round burst that didn't even come close to hitting the merc's would-be target.

A nine-round pattern from the flame-belching MINIMI M249 light machine gun caught the hardguy just above the belt line, hacking him into two pieces just as effectively as a machete, only a whole lot messier. As the upper torso crashed to the ground with its arms outstretched, nerve impulses fired to the legs a microsecond before death caused the blood-spurting lower body to take a few jerky steps. Then it too toppled over.

Death spasms continued to jerk the trigger hand, firing off the last few rounds in the subgun's mag to puncture the four-by-four's tires on the side closest to the corpse.

Phoenix strode over to the armored personnel carrier and four-by-four, both painted a military olive-drab and bearing the Sheik's coat of arms—a desert eagle holding automatic weapons in its claws.

He turned and looked for the family he had rescued, but could see no sign of them. Big Wally, on the other hand, was highly visible. The little man seemed to be circulating excitedly through the crowd of bystanders. Trench could see street scavs handing the midget money, probably in payment on a bet on Trench's chances of survival.

He swung back around to face the Sheik's personnel carrier and slung the MINIMI over his shoulder. Removing the HK "Granatpistole" 40-mm personal grenade launcher, and loading it with an incendiary high-explosive round, Trench stepped back and fired point-blank into the tracked vehicle's hindquarters.

The APC's gas tank ruptured as the grenade detonated on impact. A fireball went up with a loud *whoosh* as searing hot air expanded to crash against the cooler air on the periphery of the fireball. Secondary explosions from the fuel lines as they caught fire sent the front end of the half-track up in jagged pieces of twisted steel wreckage. The vehicle's remains sailed down in a grim aerial ballet of flaming metal fragments.

The man in the center of the vortex stood his ground, as if knowing that the potentially lethal shards of razor-sharp steel could hurt him as little as flakes of winter snow.

The roar of engines signaled the approach of more attack vehicles. Trench had expected them. He readied the MINIMI with a fresh 40-round clip and wielded the reloaded HK grenade pistol in his free hand. Let the mothers come. Trench was ready.

Instead of riding in with cannons blazing, they were showing the white flag.

The badass waving it approached cautiously from the lead four-by-four vehicle, his black eyes wavering between the MINIMI and HK barrels and Trench's eyes, as if unsure of which posed the greatest threat. All looked equally lethal to the punk.

The punk's knees were knocking as he approached the man with the action-primed weapons and the flint-gray eyes.

"Spit it out, puppy dog," Trench said.

"T-the   Shuh-Sheik,"   the   emissary stammered. "H-he wants to muh-meet you."

"Give me one good reason why I should meet him."

The emissary trembled even harder now. "H-he says to look over there for your answer." The punk pointed behind him and to his left.

The .50-caliber Browning machine guns of a Piranha light-armored tank were trained on the crowd of rubbernecking bystanders.

One of the khaki-suited Royal Guardsmen held a long-barreled SMG to Big Wally's head. The midget was kicking in the air as the merc held him up off the ground with the other hand on the collar of his western shirt.

Trench holstered the HK and lowered his MINIMI light machine gun, just enough to signal he intended no immediate threat but not too low to prevent raising the lethal peacemaker to action position on a heartbeat's notice.

"You call the shots," he told the shivering emissary, who seemed on the verge of tears of gratitude now that the deadly automatic weapons were no longer aimed point-blank at his face.

"For now."

8

"Announcing His Ultra-Highness, Sheik Abdullah X. Shabbaz, Lord High Master of the City of Las Vegas." The punk was a little guy dressed up like a cross between Rudolph Valentino and the Witch of Endor. He wore a big white turban with a peacock feather pinned to its front, green felt shoes with pointy tips, and a red silk shirt with balloon sleeves. Standing beside the Sheik's throne, he read to the audience from a scroll in his hands.

The Sheik's throne room was located in the former Omnimax Cinema of Caesar's Palace. On the vast dome, largely undamaged by nuclear blast, were projected images of thick, fleecy clouds, illuminated by the fiery disk of a rising sun. An angelic choir sang the praises of the Sheik by way of a megawatt sound system.

Reached by one of the remaining three of the hotel's original 24 high-speed elevators, the Sheik's throne room occupied the topmost penthouse floor of the 60-story structure—the Empire State Building of Las Vegas.

On a banner hung above the throne was the

Sheik's motto. It was a line from *Little Caesar*:

Whom he couldn't corrupt, he terrified.
Whom he couldn't terrify, he murdered.

The Sheik had always liked that one.

Maybe the Sands or the Dunes might have been more appropriate namewise. But Caesar's was the best Vegas had to offer, so the Sheik had taken it for himself. Under new management, it was now officially known as the Royal Palace of Las Vegas.

A bevy of royal bimbos attired in sexy harem outfits attended the Sheik at his throne. Some lounged on huge satin pillows, toking from bubbling glass hookahs, while others wielded enormous ostrich-feather fans to waft the air around their gaudily attired master or dropped delicacies of various kinds into his lordly mouth.

"He whose infinite mercy makes possible the rising and setting of the sun and moon," the Sheik's effeminate mouthpiece went on. "He whose generosity knows no bounds and whose vision penetrates beyond the most infinite reaches of space and time and deep into the hearts and souls of all men. He whose wrath is terrible yet whose compassion and mercy to all flow as deep as the waters of the life-giving ocean. He whose—"

The chatter of autofire made the fag almost jump out of his turban. The chamber resounded with peals of laughter.

"That will be enough, Shades," came the Sheik's voice. "You may go now."

Shades struggled to re-roll the scroll he had been reading from. An expertly aimed dagger whizzed by his face, almost close enough to give him a shave—had he any facial hair, that is.

Shades shrieked girlishly and ran from the throne room like a bat out of hell, trailing the scroll behind him and leaving the Sheik's chamber echoing with whistles and applause.

One guy in the Sheik's audience wasn't amused by the fag or impressed by the Sheik's big buildup.

Like the man said, the cheaper the crook, the gaudier the patter. That went double for the clothes.

The big guy with the corded biceps stood before the throne of the Sheik. He was fully armed and his weapons and ammo gave him the appearance of some invincible machine of destruction, far more dangerous than a mere human being.

The throne room's occupants could believe that. Especially after the performances they'd seen him turn in—against the Sheik's army in the Casino Center firefight that had gotten him brought here, and before that in the squared circle of the Circus Maximus against Og Magog.

They gave him a wide berth.

The Sheik motioned toward Phoenix.

"On your knees before His Ultra-Highness," one of the Sheik's Royal Guardsmen growled, motioning floorward with the barrel of his SMG.

A 7.62-mm frag round knocked the badass off his feet before he even knew what hit him. His last earthly vision was a wisp of smoke curling from the barrel of an Uzi SMG that had moved so fast he hadn't even seen it raised.

His pards in paramilitary khaki took up battle positions, ready to start throwing lead at the Sheik's signal.

"Ah . . . look," said Big Wally to Trench, standing beside him. "Maybe you better let me do the talking from here on in. Okay, champ?"

Big Wally rolled his eyes. This clown was going to get them both snuffed. Clamping a fat stogie firmly between his jaws, the midget strode through the ranks of kill-hungry badasses until he stood before the throne.

Propping one leg on the top step of the dais on which the throne stood, Big Wally began. "See, it's like this, Sheik, I am Mr.—" He realized he didn't know the dude's name and called to Trench. "Hey, exactly what is your name anyway, Kemo Sabe?"

Trench told him.

"Right," Big Wally went on. "I'm Mr. Trench's representative, manager, confidant, and legal adviser, see? You gotta understand, Sheik, Mr. Trench don't like to be crowded.

"If you wanna do business, that's fine, but we gotta talk man to man. My client ain't just a common punk, you know."

"Ah yes, Mr. Trench is obviously not a man who takes kindly to threats," the Sheik said after a moment's reflection, waving off his goons. The mouth-breathers returned to their positions flanking the throne, looking vaguely disappointed. "He demands courtesy." The Sheik looked directly at Trench. "Approach me, if you will, sir."

"You forgot to say please," Trench said.

Big Wally gestured frantically and shook his head.

The Sheik's face colored slightly. If he was mad, he barely showed it. "By all means, please. Even pretty please. With Colombian cocaine on top, if you wish."

Yeah, Trench thought to himself as an amused smile played across his lips. A punk by any other name... Stepping up he saw the pockmarks in the Sheik's face. The brocade cape, emblazoned with his phony coat of arms, the ridiculous turban, the jeweled scepter, and all the other hokey trappings—including the mirrored aviator shades—didn't make him appear any less of a punk. You could dress them up, but they still reeked of something about to get flushed.

Suddenly a couple of bandaged dudes broke from the ranks and sprinted for the throne. Trench didn't recognize them, but their injuries made it a good bet that they'd come from Trinity.

"He's the motherfucker who burned us!" one of them shouted, cowering every time he glanced Trench's way.

"Yeah, we demand retribution, Sheik!" the other added. "This guy here trashed the town singlehandedly. Just breezed in and attacked all us peace-loving citizens."

The Sheik nodded. "You see, Mr. Trench, I am responsible for the entire southwestern quadrant of this state. Trinity pays me a yearly tribute of one million dollars in gold. In return, I offer them protection.

"In addition, you have taken the lives of some of my most trusted men and destroyed military vehicles worth hundreds of thousands of dollars, to say nothing of endangering the safety of those who have come to Las Vegas to attend the Murder Marathon, relying on my munificence and loving-kindness to make their sojourn safe as well as enjoyable."

"That's a laugh," Trench returned. "You call your goons dragging a woman away to be raped safe and enjoyable? If it is, I'd hate to see your idea of dangerous and unpleasant."

The Sheik's face clouded over. A smirk played over the thin lips beneath the mirrored eyeglass frames. "Pray that you never do, Mr. Trench," he intoned ominously. Then his face lightened. "What exactly precipitated the breakneck vehicular chase through the Desert of Fire?"

"There was a difference of opinion," Trench returned.

"Regarding what, may I ask?"

"A man sold me some gasoline. He was the kind of guy for whom selling something once isn't good enough. So he sent some punks to take back his merchandise. I put those punks underground. End of story."

"Ah, but you're mistaken, Mr. Trench."

At a snap of his fingers, one of the Sheik's entourage opened a metal box and removed a small mechanical device. The Sheik pointed it in Trench's direction. It emitted a shrill series of high-pitched tones.

"This is a CAM molecule sniffer. It is identical to the ones carried by Immune bounty hunters. It was a group of bounty hunters that started the conflict, not the good people of Trinity." He put the CAM aside. "And I can see why. Those readings indicate you are quite a valuable commodity, Mr. Trench."

What the Sheik also knew was that Trench and Phoenix were one and the same. The CAM readings confirmed it. SCORF had issued an all-points Priority Alert informing all the feudal lords of the Southwest of the general description of the man wanted by US-NCSC Government forces.

They had been vague on precisely why, but the Sheik's sources had confirmed that Phoenix was some kind of supermerc who had single-handedly wiped out an entire Government installation with a tactical nuke. Common sense told the Sheik that the man called Phoenix was now standing right in front of him.

"There's a price on your head, *Phoenix*—that is what you're called, right?"

Trench was silent. He sized up the opposition, looking for escape routes. They had made a bad mistake in allowing him possession of his weapons. The odds weren't good, but they were workable.

"I should turn you over, but we may be able to do business," the Sheik went on.

"I don't do deals with punks," Trench returned.

Big Wally quickly jumped between Phoenix and the Sheik.

"Hold on, Kemo Sabe," he interjected. "Let's hear His Ultra-Highness out. After all, what have we got to lose?"

"I *need* a superman, Trench." The Sheik looked around him. "You don't know of our Murder Marathon, do you?" He held up a hand. "No, you obviously don't.

"The Murder Marathon is more than just a stock-car race. It is even more than just a gladiatorial contest on wheels. The Murder Marathon is a trial by combat determining the legitimate destiny of those factions the drivers represent. If one fails, all of those he duels in the name of fail as well.

"Las Vegas needs a champion. I think you may be the driver for whom we've been searching. In return for agreeing to the honor of representing her in the Murder Marathon, Las Vegas will reward you with ten thousand dollars in gold."

"And what if I don't?" Trench asked.

"Then I will slaughter one hundred innocents for every day you continue to withhold your agreement. And I will personally deliver you to SCORF—in pieces so small they won't even make noise when they drop."

"Fuck you," Trench told him.

"Good," the Sheik returned, appearing pleased with himself. "Then we have a deal."

One thing about the Sheik of Las Vegas—he was a guy who knew the meaning of the word hospitality. The royal suite he'd given Trench might have been under heavy guard, but as a cage it was as gilded as they came.

The bedroom had a mirrored ceiling over a heart-shaped water bed, lime draperies, and a wet bar. But for Trench, the best part of the suite was its passion-purple tiled bathroom with a working shower. This was the first shower with hot and cold running water Trench had taken since he'd left the San Francisco Hilton for a week of badly needed isolation and spiritual replenishment in Golden Gate National Park. That week had ended in a waking nightmare when the nukes had dropped. Keeping the MINIMI propped within fast-grabbing distance, he alternated with hot and cold streams of water, washing the Mojave Desert dust of his body.

Trench was so wrapped up in it that he almost didn't hear the sounds of padded footsteps as intruders stole into the bedroom beyond.

Keeping the shower running, Trench silently picked up the formidable SAW weapon, glad he'd cranked a high-velocity hollowpoint round into the chamber in the event of just such a contingency.

Holding the MINIMI at navel level, its black, bell-shaped muzzle drawing an instant bead on the targets in the room beyond, Trench kicked open the bathroom door.

Two harem lovelies, clad scantily in merry widows, garter belts, and high stockings with

spike-heeled pumps, shrieked in panic as they
were confronted by the naked guy clutching the
ultimate symbol of male potency.

"Hey! Watch where you point that thing,
mister!" one of the Sheik's sluts protested.

Trench put the Megastopper down. Yeah, the
Sheik was some kind of a host all right. First a
hot shower and now two hot little ladies. By
anybody's standards, these two were the cream.

They looked like former porn starlets and
seemed to be Immunes, their milk-white bodies
without a mark on them. Except for a crescent-
shaped brand above their right ankles you only
saw if you looked closely. That would be the
Sheik's brand, identifying them as his personal
sexual chattel.

"Do you two have names?" Trench asked,
admitting that the sight of his host's nubile
nymphets aroused his lusts. The girls smiled.
They were on familiar turf now. The symbol of
manhood they now saw standing in erect appre-
ciation of their feminine charms was the kind
they had never had any difficulty coping with.

"I'm Royce," the blonde pro with the jutting
breasts tipped by nipples the size of cigar stubs
said. Ivory was the name of her slightly taller,
slightly slimmer, but every bit as eye-pleasing
partner with straight black hair that fell to her
alabaster shoulders.

Royce and Ivory knelt at Trench's erect rod,
their tongues and lips and fingers teasing and
coaxing it to the full brink of arousal. When they
could sense the nearness of onrushing orgasm,
they released him and took up positions on the
bed, ready for sexual play.

While the blonde lay with her legs spread
wide to receive the brunette's head between them,
the brunette crouched with her tight little ass

jacked in the air, feeling Trench grasp her by her narrow waist and begin to fill her with his deep thrusting hardness.

"Now, damn you!"

The man staring into the TV monitor beside the Sheik of Las Vegas had the erect bearing of a soldier, but the cold psycho fire in his pale-blue eyes was a telltale sign that he was a soldier of fortune.

The vintage World War II Mauser bearing the death's-head emblem of the Nazi SS Sonder-kommando slung across his chest in a pit-holster confirmed this impression.

John Tallon derived a warped pleasure as he watched Phoenix's sex organ reduce the savviest whores in Vegas to quivering human jelly. Those two little man-eaters were totally out of control, coming as though they were about to choke on their own passion while that pistoning cock rammed them, again and again and again. The merc balled his fists until his knuckles whitened.

"I give the orders here, SCORF man," the Sheik countered. "And I say we kill him when he's fulfilled his commitment."

The Sheik flicked off the monitor.

"Remember that you need me to help keep this sector under control," he went on. "I deliver the goods, Tallon. Enoch knows that. *You* know that. I need Trench alive, at least until the end of the Murder Marathon. After that, he's all yours."

Tallon stared into the reflecting surfaces of the Sheik's sunglasses with his penetrating manic gaze. Behind the lenses he could faintly discern the blistered retinal tissues of a nuclear-blast victim. The Sheik was right, the merc knew.

Without his control, the entire Southwest Corridor would be in danger of being overrun by

badasses, Contams, and zombie scavs from Los
Angeles. That city was a real cesspool, and only
298 miles away. SCORF command had declared it
TDZ, a totally destroyed zone. L.A. was like a big
zoo without keepers, where animals were eating
each other alive.

But having the Phung Hoang so close was
almost unbearable. In his mind he saw himself
blowing Trench away, dismembered limbs and
ripped-off body parts hitting the walls with wet,
sloppy sounds. . . .

"After the Murder Marathon, Tallon," the
Sheik repeated. "Then you get the Alpha-
Immune."

Yeah, thought Tallon.

Then you might just get something too.

A slight case of sudden death.

9

In a country of the blind, the Sheik asked himself, a one-eyed man was what?

The answer was simple. He was the guy who held all the aces.

Whereas beneath the muscle and firepower of the man called Phoenix was the fatal flaw of giving a damn about anybody besides Numero Uno. His life-risking response to the staged abduction in the Bermuda Triangle had shown the Sheik how he could put Phoenix in his pocket. Since the Sheik owned everybody and everything else in town, why shouldn't he own Phoenix too?

Ah, but it hadn't always been that cut and dried. Back in Detroit, Vince Sators had been just another two-bit punk with a couple of interstate warrants for petty beefs hanging over him. Hooked up with the Aryan Brotherhood biker gang during a prison stretch at Almira State Penitentiary, Sators had soon been connected with the Mafia kingpins who ran Las Vegas and occasionally contracted out to free-lance enforcers.

Quickly moving up the ladder, Vince had

become head honcho in the outlaw biker gangs that took orders from the Italian Mob, performing those acts the recently respectable "businessmen" had contracted out to free-lancers.

Businessmen who—like the corporate entities their smart lawyers and money men had created to present a facade of legitimacy to a gullible public—had been still as corrupt as the Bugsy Siegels, the Lucky Lucianos, and the other legendary crime bosses who'd erected a neon shrine to gambling, vice, and hedonism from the pitiless rock of the arid desert floor.

Drugs, prostitution, extortion, contract hits, money-laundering, payola—Vince Sators had had a finger in all the illicit action of the Sovereign State of Nevada's answer to Sodom and Gomorrah.

Until, like those biblical Cities of the Plain, hellfire from the skies had consumed the high-rollers' mecca with a nuclear judgment-call raining down with a wail of twisted metal and screaming pandemonium that had turned the gamblers' paradise into a suburb of hell in a flash of incinerating white heat.

In the leadership vacuum that followed, the Sheik of Vegas had iced the Mafia honchos for whom he'd played the errand boy. Cut off from their main power bases back East, the Mob God-fathers and their crews of buttonmen went down like paper targets in a shooting gallery. "Businessmen" couldn't sweat the new heat rising in radioactive waves from the flash-fused desert sands.

Only warriors could.

A new breed of killers with hearts of steel and souls of fire. Strongmen to whom nothing but crushing everything weaker and smaller than themselves was the prime motivating force behind existence. Badassed wielders of heavy metal, motorized madmen hell-bent on riding hard and dying young.

Such was the human wreckage from which the Sheik had molded his elite Royal Guardsmen.

After exterminating the Mob kingpins, the Sheik's crew had fought a short, hard battle against rival gangs of badass survivors for control of the southwestern quarter of Nevada. But coming from the biggest power base in the nuclear deathzone had placed the overwhelming odds on the side of the Sheik.

Those Mafiosos he'd allowed to live had turned over their vast wealth and weapons armories to him, and it gave him pleasure to think that Emilio "the Spider" Tarantola, former Mob kingpin of Vegas, was now his second in command, with his army of Mob buttonmen answering only to the Sheik.

In a few months, Vegas had emerged as a new Babylon, reigning over Hellhole, Trinity, Meltdown, Nazareth, and other towns in the nuke-scorched hotzone, exacting tribute in money, gold, weapons, women, and slave labor.

Just as serfs in the Middle Ages would flee within the walls of their lord protector's estate when danger threatened, so in this new American feudalism the Sheik would give his subjects protection from Contams, pillaging merc groups, Immune bounty hunters, and even the US-NCSC Government. In return for their warlord's protection, the Sheik's serfs would owe him their very lives.

To use a gambler's metaphor, Vegas was the only game in town. Los Angeles was a mass graveyard, hermetically sealed by Government troops. Rumor had it that the city would soon be razed to the ground, along with its sister scumhole on the East Coast, New York City.

But the Sheik knew firsthand how heavy the head that wore the crown could hang. His people needed bread and circuses. Like Nero, he figured that games released energy in a way less dangerous to him personally. Being Westerners, Las Vegans loved cars and guns. And so the Sheik had hit on the perfect way of letting their pent-up fury loose in a productive manner.

The Murder Marathon.

Each of the surrounding towns would send their champions to represent them. These men would be the finest drivers they could produce, not only skilled in handling a car but masters of weapons as well.

He'd gotten the idea from *Ben-Hur*—chariot races in the Rome of the Caesars. That and reading about how the Romans used to flood the Colosseum and stage mock naval battles when they got tired of seeing gladiators snuffed in the arena. Up to thirty triremes, biremes, and other ships would be manned by slaves who, chained to their oars, went down with the losing teams. Sometimes the death toll had reached as high as three thousand drowned corpses.

Equipped with spikes and swords, they would fight until all were sunk except the winner. Sometimes the bloody battles had lasted for days on end. It was perfect. Except that, in Vegas, water was as scarce as sand was plentiful. So the Sheik would use cars.

No, the Romans didn't fuck around. And neither did the Sheik.

The vehicles themselves would be more than just ordinary cars. Much more. Turbocharged, armor-plated, and armed-to-the teeth road monsters. The weapons each entry carried would be limited only by the ingenuity and resources of those who equipped them. Death-on-wheels, the cars and their drivers would be sent out to wage a high-velocity death-struggle on a ten-mile track.

A battle that would end when only one of the contestants was left alive.

There would be no ties allowed in the Murder Marathon. No losers. At least no *live* losers. As somebody once remarked, it would be a conflict which did not determine who was right so much as who was *left*.

The Murder Marathon's single rule would be that only one wheelman survived. One and one only.

The winner would walk. All the others would feed the buzzards, the scorpions, and the snakes.

Sure, Phoenix was good. The Sheik had personally watched his practice runs on the racetrack, observing how he handled Death Wings, the Vegas road machine, as though the specially weaponed and armored TransAm were an extension of his own body. From what the Sheik had seen, he was satisfied that Phoenix had Cadillac Jack beat by lights years. He could be the best.

It was just his bad luck that, regardless of how the Murder Marathon went down, the life expectancy of the Phoenix man was less than zero.

The lady's name was Death Wings.

And she handled like a darkfire dream.

She was a black '87 Firebird TransAm with 427 horses under the hood, a Hurst four-on-the-floor, and a custom-installed Schliefer clutch. Her carburetor had been replaced with a Transstar X-80 exhaust system, the block bored to a reverse-lock 400-cam ratio for an extra performance margin.

The TransAm rode on heavy Michelin radials cushioned by high-speed shocks and Traction Masters controlled by a rack-and-pinion steering system with the Pitman arm geared down to a two-to-two ratio.

As a girl with something extra, Death Wings also sported a nitrogen-rich fuel-mixture switch-button mounted below the tach to give her extra power in emergency speed situations.

Sophisticated weapons systems made Death Wings a lady that packed a mean punch. There were .50-caliber machine-gun ports on the front and rear bumpers that gave her the firepower of an M-1 tank. The TransAm was also outfitted with rocket-launching tubes on its roof which could be rotated in independent 360-degree arcs using a mini-joystick on the fire-control panel.

Each of the two bundles of rocket tubes, containing ordnance with a range of 300 yards and armor-busting warheads, was designed to launch ten rockets. The fire-command control was an array of soft-touch pads mounted on a panel above the hump of the power-train emplacement between the TransAm's bucket seats, just forward of the gearshift for easy reach. The armament package also included a stud that released heavy black oil smoke for evasive maneuvers.

Death Wings was armored with layers of high-tungsten steel. Her windows had been removed and replaced with heavy wrought-iron waffling, with reinforced circular gunports to the lower right and left of the windshield.

She was a road machine built for death, not comfort.

A 25-block stretch of Vegas real estate

between Tropicana Avenue and Flamingo Road
that had once been the site of the University of
Nevada—before the party ' school had been
reduced to nuclear embers—was now a bulldozed
stretch of naked desert.

In the center of this dead zone, a circle of
rusting junkers and other wreckage had been
arranged to form a track, within which the
Murder Marathon wheelman would hone his
mobile skills before the start of the tournament.

The time: early morning. Trench put the
TransAm through its paces on the track and was
convinced that it was capable of surviving
anything that might come up against it. This
baby would have to. The TransAm was his ticket
out of Vegas.

For a long time after he and September Song
had escaped the ruins of San Francisco, Trench
had been certain that Tallon had finally brought it.
After all, the micronuke had blown his SCORF
superbase to hell in a sub-kiloton mushroom
cloud.

But lately he'd felt something gaining on
him. Some sixth sense, some psychic radar, some
hidden telepathy of Warrior Homo Sapiens, told
him that John Tallon was still alive. And Trench
knew enough about the merc's pathological
hatred of him to be certain of one thing. As long
as Tallon was breathing, he'd be gunning for his
ass.

Trench would bet on it.

The only chance for Trench to keep living was
to keep moving. Fast and hard. Being pinned
down in Vegas practically invited the
executioners from SCORF. It was even money
that the Sheik had already contacted Tallon or, if
the merc were really dead, whoever was now in
charge of SCORF Regional Command. Luther

Enoch wanted the Alpha-Immune antibodies he carried in his spinal tissue too badly not to have put all his forces on full alert. It was only the Murder Marathon, Trench realized, that was buying him time.

Trench had to use that time to plan his escape.

The Murder Marathon was the key. To be held at the Yucca Flats, 20 miles outside of Vegas, it would give him a slim chance at burning rubber out of the Sheik's desert madhouse.

By trashing the opposition, he'd render the Sheik's mass-execution threat a no-win scenario. When Trench survived the death race, the Sheik would be in no position to start blowing people away. His leverage over Trench would be a thing of the past.

At which point, Trench would have to use every ounce of speed and every deadly option the Firebird TransAm was equipped with to make a clean, fast break on a last-ditch run for his life.

"Here, honey, have another snort. Big Wally's got just the thing for what ails you."

The naked slut's eyes were already crossed, but she eagerly powdered her nose with the remaining line of coke from the mirror the midget had produced.

"Feel better now," Big Wally continued, "right, babe?"

"Oooh," the slut, whose name was Venice DeVille, said. "I feel all sparkly-warkly."

"Goodsy-woodsie," Big Wally mimicked in answer. "Now, be a good little slut and run by me again about that guy the Sheik said for you to be nice to."

"You mean the weird dude?" Venice asked. "The guy into tying people up and making them—"

"Yeah, yeah, that's the guy, "Big Wally broke in. "Make with the mouth, Venice baby."

"Well," the whore said, rolling her eyes contemplatively, "he had on this uniform with a patch on the sleeve, like—" She drew a picture of the SCORF insignia with her fingertip on the bedsheet.

"Where was this at, Venice honey?" Big Wally asked.

"Out by the airport. You know, McCarran. They have a whole military thing going on out there. Trucks, jeeps, helicopters, even a Government jet on the runway. The guy's quarters were in this prefab building, like the kind they used to have for tennis courts, and when I asked him why he didn't come up to the Sheik's palace for a girl, he said he had to keep a low profile. That's all, except for the fucking part, which—"

"That's okay, babe," Big Wally cut in. "You told me plenty. Just do Big Wally a favor, okay? If you ever go out there again, I want you to check out a couple of things. There's a yard in it for you, by the way." Venice nodded and Big Wally told her what he wanted to know about.

"Now, I want you to show me exactly what you did with that dude," Wally said, straddling the whore's face. "That's right, Venice, I said *show* me, not *tell* me."

10

Crackkkkkk!

The pistol shot reverberted across the crowded bleachers of the thronged viewing stands as the red Very flare streaked into the sky.

The Murder Marathon was about to begin.

Fierce sun beat down on the wooden bleachers that rose in crowded tiers at one end of the racetrack's course, its circumference delineated by junkers piled into a makeshift barrier. Wooden stunt ramps were positioned here and there on the racecourse for automotive acrobatics. But their purpose was not for showboating: jumping a line of burning wrecks might be the only way for a wheelman to save his neck.

In his special box close to the action, the Sheik of Las Vegas handed the flare pistol to one of his gaudily attired royal retainers and watched as the contestant vehicles circled the track, one by one, before the Murder Marathon began.

Each car bore the coat of arms of its sponsor on its roof so the crowd in the bleachers and the judges hovering overhead in helicopters could call the action.

In accordance with the rules of the deadly game, all the cars were stock models. No four-by-fours were allowed. Speed and driving skill were more important than brute size and raw power. But anything went where heavy weaponry, armor plating, and automotive extras were concerned. The nature of these special modifications to the stock cars were closely guarded secrets, to be revealed only during the deadly course of the Murder Marathon itself.

Ordinarily, six cars wouldn't have put on much of a show, even considering the fact that these cars were also deadly weapons. It was their wheelmen that would provide the audience with a knock-down, drag-out, bone-crunching fight to the finish. They were the best. Each was a champion in his own right, trained to survive and take down the opposition.

Depending on the Murder Marathon's outcome, each driver stood to gain a fortune.

First to scream across the Marathon's track was Phoenix in Death Wings, the Vegas Firebird TransAm. The crowd went wild, cheering and firing guns into the air as the black car bearing the Sheik's coat of arms emblazoned on its hood made its appearance.

Second was Hellhole's entry, a turbocharged Falcon equipped with deadly extras, called White Lightning. The extras included a 40-millimeter machine gun mounted on its hood and a mortar tube sticking out of its trunk.

Third was the entry from Trinity. The wheelman, Moondog Gomez, had been one of the survivors of the Desert of Fire road duel. His heavily armored Ford Mustang, equipped with .50-caliber machine-gun ports in front and in back, was ready for motorized combat. The car's name, Road Ripper.

Fourth, the yellow Cutlass LeSabre called Godscream was Devil's Pitchfork's entry. A 30-millimeter cannon protruded from the Cutlass's hood. Behind the wheel of the custom car, riding high on Hookers headers, was a crash-helmeted desperado known only as Nirvana.

Fifth was Meltdown's entry, a heavily armed '57 Chevy specially outfitted with an array of weapons, including a drum-fed .50-caliber Gatling gun on its roof, arrays of 30-millimeter mortar tubes, and grenade launchers.

The sixth and final car came from a shantytown called Crucifixion. Its entry was an unimpressive-looking Oldsmobile 98 named Armadillo that provoked the crowd to hysterical laughter. The car looked as slow and ungainly as its namesake implied.

Through the windshields of each vehicle in the circle, the drivers glared at each other, sizing up the opposition's death machinery and improvising hasty strategies of attack and defense.

Their eyes simultaneously tracked the Sheik in the reviewing stand as he again raised the Very pistol to signal the Murder Marathon's start. This time, as a dramatic touch, the cesium flare was aimed directly at a bullseye painted on the belly of a naked Las Vegan dangling upside down from a rope hanging from a 30-foot crane.

"Let the games begin!" the Sheik shouted, and fired the pistol, blowing the target to flame-broiled shreds.

Engines screamed as the screech of rubber against hard-packed earth filled the arena.

Trench went after the red Mustang from Trinity. The car was the most heavily armed of the pack. It made sense to take it out first if he could. He figured the competition would combine forces to take out the weakest first—the broken-down Olds from Crucifixion—before they turned on each other like a pack of starving rats. That was the logical scenario.

Screaming metal hot on his tail told him he wasn't dealing with logical people.

In the TransAm's rearview, the Mustang was coming straight at him. As .50-caliber autofire hiccupped from its front bumpers, the Cutlass LeSabre was closing in at three-o'clock.

Trench gritted his teeth and swore softly as the Cutlass opened fire with its four roof-mounted Gatling 50s. The four heavy-caliber machine guns were capable of incredible firepower, enough to turn his car and everything in it to metal mincemeat.

He needed being double-teamed right now like a second asshole. But Trench might have known that a fast, clean kill on the Vegas car would be too tempting to pass up, especially when Cadillac Jack's replacement wheelman was an unknown quantity and might turn out to be a pushover for a hard-driving frontal assault.

Making a sharp evasive left to get out of the firing line, Trench hit the rear machine-gun stud, the Browning 50 coughing out its lethal lead poison in a noxious metal stream. Flame erupted from the TransAm's rear as a zigzag of punctures appeared in the side of the Mustang. The car turned a sharp right to evade the final stitch in the gas tank its wheelman knew was imminent, but it was too late for anything but an epitaph.

The wheelman bailed out just as the fuel lines caught fire, flying through the air as the Mustang ignited into a fireball of yellow death-flame that shook the arena with a deafening roar. He wasn't fast enough to avoid being scorched by the wall of flame's expanding outer edge. His crash suit caught fire and he rolled in the dirt, managing to snuff the flames and stagger to his feet. Secondary explosions as the Mustang's artillery went up added to the fireworks.

Staggering to his feet, the Mustanger whipped a Colt .44-caliber Automag from a pit-holster across his chest. Standing spraddle-legged, he extended his arms, grasping the weapon tightly as he assumed a two-handed shooting stance and targeted it carefully on the Vegas TransAm. With his thumb, he flicked the fire-selector lever to deliver a three-round fragburst while aligning the Automag's sight on the right-hand side of the TransAm's windshield.

The high-velocity .357 wadcutters had enough stopping power to bore right through an engine block, and if they packed an explosive charge, they could do to the TransAm what Trench had just done to Trinity's Mustang.

Before the Automag's barrel drew a solid bead on Death Wings, Trench fired both of his front-mounted .50-caliber MGs in a withering cross-fire deathburst directly into the Mustanger's belly. Slugs hit him just above the belt line in a jagged shot pattern that punched a big hole through his midsection as an invisible hand seemed to pick him off his feet and hurl him backward through the air into the burning vehicle.

The Mustang from Trinity became the wheelman's own funeral pyre.

But the Cutlass and Chevy were still very much in the running. They had changed strategies, with the lighter, faster Cutlass darting in close, and the heavier Chevy pacing the TransAm, waiting for a clean strike for a fast kill.

At just closing in from behind, the Cutlass

pulled a fast bootlegger's turn and now screamed down at two o'clock high. Panels on the Plymouth's front dropped down, revealing a pneumatically controlled battering-ram attachment that would impale Trench like a joint of meat on a shish-kebob skewer.

The head of the battering ram was a high-speed drill, catching the sunlight as it spun at thousands of RPMs.

Trench could see the wheelman's face twisted into a snarl of kill-crazy bloodlust. The Chevy heavy couldn't resist giving him the finger as he began blasting away from twin side-mounted machine-gun ports, pinning the TransAm in a lethal double-barreled cross fire.

Wrenching the wheel hard to the left while simultaneously stomping the pedal down against the floorboards with everything he had, Trench swerved the TransAm from between the rock and the hard place just in time to avoid the Reaper's scythe, pulling a wheelie that skidded him on the edges of his two right tires through the narrow opening between the two onrushing death vehicles.

Its heavy-duty double-wishbone suspension absorbed the enormous impact as the TransAm crashed back onto all four wheels, and Trench pulled a fast figure-eight turn to bring Death Wings broadside of the Cutlass and Chevy, which had crashed head-on when their wheelmen had found only empty air between them.

The Cutlass's battering-ram spearhead had plowed through the Chevy's engine block, narrowly avoiding impaling the Chevy's wheelman. A cloud of hot steam hissed from the Chevy's ruptured radiator. The crowd booed wildly. Temporarily making the fatal error of forgetting the TransAm's deadly wheelman, the drivers of the Cutlass and Chevy turned on each other like two rabid dogs who'd forgotten their quarry in the heat of the chase.

But locked together by the impact of the collision, the only way they would be able to fight it out was to whip out automatic weapons and start blasting away.

Jumping from the Cutlass, the crash-suited wheelman pulled a grenade and lobbed it at the stricken Chevy. A loud *crump* and a blast and the roof of the Chevy was propelled high into the air.

The Cutlass's wheelman turned, clutching a Skorpion MK18 SMG he'd whipped from a shoulder holster, but couldn't find any corpse. That's because the Chevy guy had circled the wreckage and now came up behind and to the left of the Cutlass wheelman clutching a compact Remington 870 riot shotgun.

A flaming fantail of 00 lead exploded in a sickening blast of flame from the sawed-off pump gun's muzzle. The burst caught the Cutlass car jockey in the upper thigh, dissolving most of his left side into a fine red mist.

A lucky burst from the Skorpion as the mortally wounded wheelman went down firing hit the Chevy wheelman square in the head, ripping off one side of his face on the diagonal. Brains glistened for a second as the corpse pitched forward, jerking and kicking as the pump gun flew from his hands.

Stricken though he was, the Cutlass badass limped for his wheels and revved the 450-horsepower air-cooled engine, eager to get back into the action.

He never had a chance.

With the touch of a red stud below a flashing light, Phoenix unleashed a barrage of two heat-seeking missiles that streaked from Death

Wings' side turrets on a collision course with the Plymouth's cab.

An orange-red fireball ballooned from the car like some obscene incendiary toadstool as the wheelman's headless body was blown through the roof by the force of the explosion. The black, flailing center of the human torch the driver had become thrashed as it struck the ground, then lay still as the scorching heat incinerated the flesh into a crisp, black, carbonous mass.

The capacity crowd in the bleachers exploded into a frenzy of wild applause for the Murder Marathon's favorite. Thousands of Las Vegans gave Trench a standing ovation.

"*Phoe-nix!*" they cheered.

"*Phoe-nix! Phoe-nix! Phoe-nix!*"

It gave Trench a certain feeling deep inside.

A lot like nausea. Only sicker.

But Trench didn't have time for emotional analysis. Later for soul-searching. Three may have been down, but there were still two left and they were as dangerous as hell. Right *now* the name of the game was every man for himself.

Now was the time to go on the warpath and leave the moral questions for later.

Gunning Death Wings, Trench double-clutched the synchromesh transmission from neutral to third as one of the two other surviving deathmobiles—a red Falcon with a streak of flame painted across its flanks and a shark's mouth on its front grille—screamed at him, spitting out a rain of grenades from launchers on its sides and front.

The grenades detonated to either side of the TransAm, rocking the Firebird as Trench steered Death Wings through a tight corridor of deafening explosions and cascading shrapnel.

By trying for a fast kill and expending his

supply of grenades, the Falcon's wheelman had placed himself in a vulnerable position. One Trench would now make him pay dearly for. As the acrid smoke from the detonations cleared, Trench swerved the TransAm to bring its front end parallel to the left flank of the Falcon.

One well-placed rocket would finish him off. Trench locked his finger around the stickshift, his thumb hovering over the kill button.

Boom! Boom! Boom!

Three explosions in rapid succession rocked Death Wings, almost blowing her wheels out from under her. Without having to look, Trench knew the Olds from Crucifixion had blindsided him with some heavy artillery. Digital control displays lit up the TransAm's high-tech dash like a Christmas tree. Whether or not the hit was bad enough to cripple the car, it had given the Falcon enough time to haul ass out of the killing ground.

The Falcon burned rubber for the other end of the arena, leaking a dark trail of gas, to wait out the outcome and perform emergency repairs. Unfortunately for the Hellhole entry, the bad Olds guy permanently clipped the Falcon's wings by salting its tail with a burst of .50-caliber lead. The gas trail became a line of flame that shot up the Falcon's ass and sent it skyward in a fiery balloon. The Olds car jockey wanted no third parties. He wanted the fight strictly between himself and the Vegas wheelman.

At least this meant Trench wasn't about to get double-teamed again. If the Crucifixion wheelman wanted a brawl, he would get one. Trench jammed the stick forward and laid down the LAW with enough armor-busting firepower the Olds 98's way to blow Crucifixion's wimp entry out of existence.

There was a surprise waiting for Phoenix

when the smoke cleared.

The rockets only blew away the Olds' patched-looking outer fiberglas shell, skillfully painted to resemble rusted metal, revealing a boiler-plated exterior that hadn't even been scratched.

Now Trench knew why the Olds was called "Armadillo."

He could hear the roar of powerful turbo-charged V-8 engines as the road machine accelerated toward him on wide-tread Firestones and see the stuttering flashes of a heavy-caliber Gatling gun, blitzing out hundreds of lethal rounds per second.

The sight brought new meaning to the word "outmaneuvered."

11

Muscular memory took over as Trench's lightning reflexes hurled his body sideways and flattened it across the seat cushions. A few bare inches of airspace between him and the meat-grinding fragments of glass and metal produced by the saturation-fire hits that sheared the roof clean off the TransAm made all the difference in the world. It was as wide as the gulf between life and death.

Spinning like a flying top, the TransAm's roof frisbeed the air at incredible speed. It became a gigantic flying buzzsaw, decapitating scores of onlookers in the bleachers with the force of its momentum.

"Cocksucker spaniel!" snarled the Armadillo's wheelman. He'd hoped for a quick, clean kill to put Vegas' hot-shit stickman away for keeps.

The Crucifixion wheelman had hung back watching, striking the Vegas car when the driver had been preoccupied with the lead-spitting Falcon from Hellhole. This Vegas dude, it was plain, was too damn slick to take headon.

All the firepower or horsepower in the world wouldn't make a damn's worth of difference against the TransAm fastgunner without the element of surprise behind it.

The badass in the Olds realized that he'd just blown that element to kingdom come.

Inside his fireproof crash suit, behind the wheel of an air-cooled mobile man-eater with 800 horses under the hood, with enough heavy artillery at his fingertips to nail a battalion, the stickman felt naked and vulnerable.

"Be dead," he snarled at nobody in particular. His eyes were riveted on the roofless TransAm sitting motionless in the center of the track. *"Please be dead!"*

Movement from within the still-intact TransAm told the wheelman he was wrong again.

Covered with a layer of glass fragments, Trench sat up and gunned the engine. The V-8 caught, but didn't turn over. He twisted the key in the ignition again, but again the engine just sputtered and died.

The bad Olds guy's unshaven face lit up. "Tough luck sucker," he spat as he saw the Vegas car stalling. The punk's fingers swiveled the twin 40-mm Gatlings into firing position. He jabbed the firing stud and cut loose with a blazing arc of heavy-caliber destruction at the immobilized target vehicle.

Trench heard the engine scream to life and put the pedal to the metal.

The TransAm was gone.

Thick black smoke obscured the Firebird's true position on the Murder Marathon track. The Olds wheelman could hear its powerful engines roar somewhere in the stinking billows of diversionary smoke, but couldn't see the TransAm.

Suddenly, it appeared right in front of him.

Steel-jacketed lightning flashed from its forward gun ports, kicking up gouts of sand as the Olds stickman tore ass and burned rubber out of the strike zone. Fast wheels and desperate double-clutching jackrabbited the Armadillo out of range of the lead tornado that chewed up the blacktop inches behind its retreating fenders.

The customized Oldsmobile was one hell of a fast car, but the TransAm was just as fast. It stuck to the Armadillo's ass as if it were glued there.

Phoenix smiled as he matched the Olds wheelman zig for zig and zag for zag. The punk was good, he had to give him that. Anybody else would have been snake food by now. Crucifixion had obviously sunk a lot of money and talent into its entry in the Murder Marathon.

They'd be a force to be reckoned with in the region, or at least wanted to be.

The two surviving vehicles chased each other around the track, locked together in a hot-wheeled fight to the finish that each wheelman knew would leave one of them a corpse. Both vehicles had depleted most of their available ammo and couldn't afford to waste any shots on gun-and-run maneuvers. Both had sustained damage which, though not crippling, had nevertheless reduced the efficiency of man and machinery.

Trench held his fire as flame sporadically blossomed from the rear .40-caliber gun ports of the customized Olds, conserving his weapons reserves until he was in range of a clean shot.

For the moment, he'd wear down the Olds wheelman in a battle of wits, guts, and driving skill. Again, the Olds fastgunner had plenty of them, but Trench took a backseat to no man in that department.

"You're good and fast, junior," he growled to himself. "But I'm better and faster."

Despite the massive injuries it had suffered when the TransAm's roof had flown into the stands, the crowd went wild as the two finalist crash cars screamed crazily across the vast arena, kicking up dirt and pulling wheelies to avoid obstacles.

They had seen their share of stunt driving in their day, but the precision maneuvers the TransAm and the Olds were putting on made all the rest look second-rate.

Cadillac Jack had been good. In fact, he'd been the best. But this new guy was better. Much, much better. He outclassed him by miles.

In his reviewing-stand box, the Sheik of Vegas almost wished Trench didn't have to die today.

The man was magnificent.

He was as slick as they came. A man the Sheik could respect—even if his principles and the Phoenix man's were a universe apart.

But as soon as the race was over, Tallon and his crew would come flying in like bats out of hell and cream the sucker. The Sheik knew that no power on earth could prevent that from happening.

The funny thing was, as much as he'd been looking forward to seeing it before, he now regretted the inevitability of Phoenix's final takedown. The dude was in a class by himself.

The speedometer needle of the Olds crashed through the redline as the turbocharged muscle-machine desperately tried to shake the TransAm that matched it move for move, stunt for stunt, yard for yard.

The wheelman wanted desperately to pull a bootlegger and get a broadside shot at the Firebird. He knew the Firebird's right side was its most vulnerable. It would only take a second. But so far, no dice.

When the wheelman zigged right, the TransAm zagged along with it. When he zagged left, the TransAm matched his lethal choreography with the precision of a high-speed motorized ballet dancer.

If the bad Olds guy used one of the wooden ramps to pull a jump, the TransAm came up right behind him, sailing through the air for a perfect four-point landing. Anybody else would have fucked up and crashed, but not this hombre. His reflexes were nothing short of inhuman.

The Olds wheelman had heard about this guy they called Phoenix. There were rumors he was some kind of superman, others that he was some kind of bionic. He could believe those rumors now, seeing the guy in action.

Any minute now, Trench thought to himself, *this guy is gonna start fucking up.*

His finger hovered lightly over the kill button for the TransAm's forward rocket tubes. When Phoenix spotted the signs of mental fatigue in the Olds stickman, he'd bear down for the big burn. Quick and clean, the Olds would be history.

Any minute—
Now!

Completing a high-speed circuit of the immense racecourse, the Olds made a beeline for the ramps. The wheelman had been using them to stage high-speed jumps; obviously they were a specialty of his.

He knew he was good at them and was daring the opposition to follow, hoping the car jockey behind him couldn't continue to match his daredevil driving. The Olds had surged ahead, gaining speed to hit the ramp at better than 100 miles per hour. The car had made it into the air and sailed over, but, instead of coming down for a perfect four-point landing, had nearly upended itself.

The Olds's wheelman had recovered, but not fast enough. In those precious seconds he had exposed his vulnerable flank to the pursuing TransAm.

Hitting the red kill button, Trench let the Olds have it with both barrels. Flame erupted in ugly devil's tongues from the machine-gun ports up front. Heavy-caliber bullets thudded into the car's blind side, opening up raw punctures as easily as if the Olds were a tin can.

"Sweet Jesus!" the wheelman spat as a glance in the rearview confirmed his death sentence. In a desperate bid to forestall the inevitable, he quickly did a two-handed rotation of the wheel, simultaneously stepping down on the gas. The Olds skidded on its own momentum, but didn't get very far before the twin death-hails struck their marks.

The bullets tearing through the Armadillo's three-inch boiler-plate skin an instant later were unwelcome signs he'd been right. One of the slugs fragmented on the engine block and ripped through his shoulder, lodging in the thick muscle of the upper back.

The Olds wheelman howled in pain as blood spurted out onto the seat. But he wasn't complaining—a moment's hesitation more and he'd have been dead meat.

The kill wouldn't be quick, Trench knew, as the Olds burned rubber away from the death zone. For that matter, it wouldn't be clean. The guy wasn't just slick, he was lucky. But he was wounded and almost out of ammo. He was finished and he knew it. It was only a matter of time before he'd be asleep for good.

The Armadillo trailed dense black smoke from its damaged carb as it performed a series of evasive maneuvers to throw the TransAm off its tail. Trench wouldn't get a second chance to catch the Olds 98 at a point of maximum vulnerability.

There would be no more flashy moves off the jump ramp.

The stricken wheelman was running for his life and would have to be taken on the run. That would be as dangerous for Trench as it would be for the bad Olds guy because at the speeds they were going there'd be no room to avoid any high-velocity steel fragments from the explosions that would inevitably occur.

Trench increased his finger's pressure on the kill button's surface. Another second and he'd let the punk have it in the rear with a high-velocity mortar round. At this range he couldn't miss, but he didn't know if he could get clear of the lethal steel debris the strike would produce either.

Then the incredible happened.

There was a sudden shriek as the Olds swerved to avoid a body which had fallen from the spectator stands above. As the car dodged around it, Trench could see that it was a small child. Trench floored the brakes, stopping a fraction of an inch from striking the child head on, but for the Olds stickman luck had just run out.

The Armadillo careened out of control, crashing into a concrete embankment, flipping over on its roof and bursting into flame with an explosion that rocked the arena and sent a wave of intense heat washing over the faces of the stunned spectators closest to the crash site.

It was over.

Phoenix climbed out of Death Wings and

picked up the child. The little girl wept in his arms as he handed her to one of the spectators in the stands.

The sound of the cheering crowd was deafening, but Trench didn't feel like a victor.

The guy in the Olds had been good.

Maybe the rest of his life had been as diseased as a cancer, but at the last moment he'd been very good. He had acted like a man, not a punk.

Trench stood staring into the burning pyre that had been the Olds, the roar of the crowd in his ears as thick, black palls of stinking smoke billowed from automotive wreckage strewn all over the Murder Marathon racecourse.

Suddenly, there was another sound rising in a raucous counterpoint to the crowd's jubilant cheers. At first Trench was too preoccupied to pay attention to it, but then his instincts warned him to turn.

When he did he saw other vehicles exiting from the starting gates. They were military HUMMERS.

The vehicles bore the interlocking-sevens emblem of elite SCORF mercs and men wielding long-barreled automatic weapons sat in them as they raced toward him at breakneck speed.

Yeah, he thought. A setup.

An instant later, the hellish sound of autofire thundered from the rapidly oncoming vehicles like a grim incendiary requiem.

12

A heavy-metal blizzard raced toward Trench at a muzzle velocity of 400 feet per second as the SCORF hit honchos opened up with everything in their mechanized arsenal.

These guys weren't taking any prisoners.

None that breathed, anyway.

However it went down, there was no way Trench would simply stand around waiting for the Reaper's scythe to cut him down. If he was going out, he'd go out the way he came in.

Fighting.

Death Wings' powerful V-8 engine screamed as the TransAm went from zero to 90 MPH in three seconds flat. Fast-cycling lead hurricaned past Trench's ears as he double-clutched the Hurst into fifth, feeling the synchromesh transmission feed RPMs to the wheels with catlike power. There was only one chance in a million for the stunt he had in mind to work. But it was the only chance there was and there was no choice but to stake everything on its success.

Between the TransAm and the squad of HUMMERS were the ramps. Behind Death

Wings, another motorized attack unit was closing the box. As Trench floored the accelerator, giving Death Wings' V-8 everything it had, he cut loose with two of his few remaining rockets at the encircling force.

A HUMMER exploded in front and behind. Men rained like flaming ants from the careening vehicles that sped on in a collision course with death, but the remaining HUMMERS were still coming on strong.

A heartbeat before he hit the ramp at 120 MPH, Trench jabbed the green button releasing the nitrogen-rich fuel mixture into the TransAm's carb.

The engine screamed as the tires RPM'd at ten times their normal velocity.

The TransAm lifted off into space, almost turning belly-up in a full vertical, and sailed 20 feet in the air over the advancing SCORF deathforce.

Death Wings crashed through the junkers separating the Murder Marathon racetrack from the spectator stands and tore through the open-air bazaar set up outside the Murder Marathon track, sending spectators scattering in all directions and knocking over the makeshift stalls of food sellers and the gaudy tents of whores.

The SCORF cowboys were still trying to figure out what hit them when the TransAm bumped and skidded across the surface of the desert, careening desperately toward the ribbon of blacktop that snaked past it, then whipping straight as an arrow toward the Arizona border.

But Trench knew he'd only bought himself a few seconds of life.

That's about all even major miracles were worth these days.

Seconds later, the telltale high-pitched

turbine scream of an F-11 attack fighter hot on his ass came as no major surprise.

Also no surprise was the fact that his gas gauge was dropping past the redline.

"Making visual contact with target vehicle now." The F-11 pilot spoke into his throat communicator.

Completely encasing the pilot's head was a wraparound helmet that gave him the appearance of a bug-eyed denizen of another solar system. Huge sensor arrays covering the front of the helmet seemed like the eyes of some immense human fly.

Inside the Visually Coupled Airborne Systems Simulator (VCASS) helmet, miniature fiber-optic screens produced a computer-generated color-graphic display of the terrain below. The F-11's "controls" were accessible to the pilot by "touching" a color-coded computer menu, also an illusion produced by VCASS.

So accurate was the fighter's onboard fire-control computer that the road-burning TransAm, the shrubbery, Joshua trees, and even automotive debris littering the highway's surface were clearly visible to the pilot, more visible even then if he had been viewing them with his naked eyes.

Overlaid above the terrain was a digitalized flight path, showing up as a flashing "slalom run" of broken green, luminous lines which effectively locked the craft and pilot onto the vehicle the man-machine interface was pursuing.

"Roger," responded a voice in the pilot's ear. "Destroy target immediately." Miles away, in the command-and-control pod of an ADATS mobile low-level air-defense (LLAD) command vehicle—nicknamed "the giraffe" for its

STENTOR search-radar banks mounted on a pneumatic "neck" with a span of 30 feet—Tallon was directing the fighter's pursuit of the TransAm. Trench was too dangerous to remain alive.

SCORF techs would be able to salvage enough of what was necessary to perform a bone-marrow implant from even the smallest surviving human remains. A single cell scraping would be sufficient. Why bother with the rest?

"Closing on target vehicle now," the pilot responded, reviewing the most effective weapons options for destroying the TransAm, which showed up as a red blip flashing across the bottom perimeter of the slalom-run overlay. He decided to use one of the underwing launchable STINGER missiles to make the kill. The pilot had been briefed on the importance of the Immune's tissues surviving the kill and had incorporated this req into his formula for destruction.

The STINGER would neutralize the vehicle and cause minimal damage to the corpse.

The pilot might even earn himself a medal for this one. It would look good on his uniform on a hot Vegas weekend.

Trench swerved the TransAm in a zigzagging series of escape maneuvers he knew wouldn't do much good against the highly maneuverable and heavily armed F-11 supersonic fighter.

His only chance was finding some cover. Because of the nature of its target, the fighter was forced to fly low in a ground-hugging flight path that would limit its effectiveness to relatively flat, open terrain. This made it imperative for the pilot to score a hit before the TransAm reached the line of jagged mountains beginning a few miles away.

At the 160 MPH Trench was doing in the howling TransAm, he'd reached the point where the highway would begin to slice through the side of a mountain in a matter of minutes. Yet, as close as relative safety was, there was little chance of his reaching it in time with the heavily armed fighter harrying him like a hawk chasing a jackrabbit.

What good were minutes when only seconds lay between you and fiery death? With each tick of the clock, death was inching nearer. In a few ticks more, Trench knew, the pilot would fire one of the lethal missiles mounted beneath the fighter's wings, and it would be all over but for the wording of his epitaph.

Time was stretched thin, attenuating like a fiber of platinum drawn through a white-hot flame.

Trench rotated the firing tubes mounted on either side of Death Wings' sculptured metal flanks and hit the launch button as the F-11's shadow slid overhead, letting fly the TransAm's final remaining rockets.

Time stood still.

Phoenix felt the explosion that seemed to lift the TransAm off the surface of the highway, like a plastic toy in a wind tunnel, before he heard its thunderous roar. His world spun around in a dizzying whirlpool as the car did a series of 360-degree flips, bursting into flame on the final roll and bathing its wheelman in a river of fire.

"Forgive me Sandra," Trench whispered as he pinwheeled through a flesh-searing kaleido-scope, staring straight ahead at its center into the black hole of death that was to be his final destination.

BOOK TWO

. . . OUT LIKE A LAMB

13

"What?" asked the Dark Messiah of his cat's-paw. "You mean he isn't dead?"

"I didn't say that," Tallon returned at the hideous, black robotic face on the console screen in the LLAD's mobile war room. "We're just not sure."

The Dark Messiah's top merc went on to explain that, while search teams deployed from the SCORF base at McCarran Airport had found human body parts among the scattered wreckage of both the Firebird TransAm and the F-11 fighter, the tissue samples were still being analyzed. Moreover, the more-than-one-mile radius over which the wreckage had been scattered had complicated the search and analysis procedures.

"But," Tallon assured Luther Enoch over the transcontinental satellite patch-through, "we have every reason to believe Phoenix was a casualty."

"Phoenix is alive," Enoch shot back angrily. "I can feel it in my guts. The man has more lives than a cat."

"We're sorting through the wreckage now," Tallon answered firmly. "We're reviewing the pilot's last tapes. Don't worry. My men will have collected enough of the Alpha-Immune's tissues for a bone-marrow transplant in a few hours."

"I'm not worried, Tallon," Enoch returned. "It's you who should be." The screen winked off, leaving John Tallon staring at utter blankness—the image of what the future held for anyone who displeased the Dark Messiah one time too many.

14

Stonehenge was just as Brian Trench had pictured it as being. In the eight-year-old's imagination, he could almost see the ghosts of the Druidic builders of the prehistoric shrine to their dark gods. It was all his father could do to keep the impulsive youngster from climbing beneath the restraining cordon of chains that the British National Trust had put up to keep the sightseers from vandalizing the incredibly ancient stone circle.

Magnus Trench was impressed himself. The arcane circle of standing stones, topped with crudely dressed lintels quarried in the human race's savage dawn, seemed even more foreboding beneath the brooding thunderheads that loomed over the windswept expanse of Salisbury Plain. He could feel the magnetism of the place and understood why those who had erected it long millennia before had considered the ground on which it stood as sacred.

Trench, Sandra, and Brian had left Victoria Station early that morning to begin a rail-and-bus

*tour that had taken them almost halfway across
England. They'd stopped at the town of Bath and
visited the underground museum built on the
ruins of an ancient Roman spa, where mineral
pools that steamed in the light drizzle were fed by
water bubbling up from natural hot springs deep
within the earth. Sandra had enjoyed seeing the
thatched roofs of the cottages in the Wiltshire
countryside, each displaying a squirrel, rabbit, or
other animal made of straw as the trademark of
its thatcher.*

"Brian, c'mere—"

*The boy had dashed under the restraining
chain before his mother could grab him and was
scuttling over the prehistoric columns of quarried
bluestone.*

*"Goddamnit, Brian, you're gonna be sorry
when your father catches up with you—"*

Sandra's sentence ended in a rising scream.

*A huge, clawed hand covered with armored
scales had erupted through the earth and
wrapped itself around the boy's torso. The ground
shook as jagged forks of lightning struck the
earth with a thunderous roar.*

*The boy struggled as the grotesque colossus
raised him high in the air. Pieces of the child's
body rained down as the monstrosity grasped the
boy by the legs and began devouring him whole,
biting off the head and most of the shoulders in a
single gulp.*

*Trench jumped over the fence and was
instantly grasped around the waist by an
enormous, sucker-covered tentacle that had
sprouted up through the ground. His final image
before his spine was crushed was of his wife.
Hands to her face, eyes wide with horror, she had
her mouth gaping open in an unending, though*

utterly silent, scream. . . .

"M-Force be praised!"

The light burned his eyes. It glowed at the end of a long tunnel surrounded by kaleidoscopic fragments of color. Slowly, the shapes at his vision's edge resolved into a rosette, like the petals of some bizarre flower. Finally, the petals became faces. Faces looking down at Trench.

"Don't try to get up," one of the faces said. "You're not ready yet."

"I'll go get the Body Tech," said another.

The speaker nodded as one of the petals/faces detached from the circle and left. Trench heard a door close. The sound echoed strangely, pinballing around in his skull. He tried to move his arms and legs and found that he couldn't.

Turning his head was agony, but it confirmed that the worst of his fears were unjustified. His limbs were still attached to his body, and though there were long lines of stitches running across his chest and stomach, he seemed otherwise intact. Thick leather restraints secured his naked body to a hospital bed.

"Get these things off," Trench said angrily. Fear was etched on the faces looking down at him. "Please," he repeated in a softer voice. "They aren't necessary anymore."

The first speaker bent and undid the restraints. Slowly, Trench raised his hands to his head and rubbed his wrists. He sat up, fighting the waves of agonizing pain and sudden nausea that coursed through him. All at once, he remembered the dream he had before he'd awakened.

The dreamscape had been familiar. It was Stonehenge, a place he'd visited the previous year on a vacation to England. Those people in the dream—the boy, the woman. They were his family. Yes? They must have been. But try as he might, he couldn't remember their names, and their faces were shrouded in the mists that obscured his memory.

For that matter, he couldn't remember much of anything prior to awakening. Tantalizing image fragments—faces, names, sounds, places—rose to the surface like ice in a churning sea, only to instantly submerge as soon as they broke the rolling waters of consciousness. They were part of a shattered mosaic of events that had brought him here . . . wherever *here* was. Yet they were as alien as the landscape of the nightmare from which he'd just awakened.

One of the group that had surrounded him when he came around—there were four of them, two women and two men, all wearing flowing white garments—brought him something cold in a plastic cup. Trench drank. It was orange juice. Frozen concentrate. The taste was instantly identifiable. The memory came easily to mind. Nevertheless, it was part of the dream, part of another lifetime.

"Thank you," Trench said, handing back the cup to the girl with long blonde hair. She smiled as she accepted it. "What's your name?"

"I am Topaz Borealis," she responded. "I am your Monitor. We've all been watching you, caring for you, hoping you'd survive the great burning." She looked away and Trench caught the faint glimmer of a tear in the girl's large blue eyes. "We thought you wouldn't make it for a while," she continued. "But now you're here with us. Alive."

"Where exactly is *here*?" Trench asked.

"Here." Topaz answered, as though the

question were superfluous. "Here in Earth-womb."

Before Trench could say any more, a fifth person entered the room. The man was young, bearded, roughly in his late 30s. He was dressed like the others, only with a red patch on the right sleeve of his white gown. He sat down on the bed beside Trench, introducing himself as Body Tech Aquarius.

"Look straight ahead," Aquarius said, shining a penlight beam into Trench's eyes. "Good," he said, nodding. The Body Tech then took his pulse and went through a series of other diagnostic tests. "Bad news," he said finally.

"Yeah? What?"

"Looks like you'll make it."

Body Tech Aquarius shook out a cigaret from a pack of Luckies and offered one to Trench. Lighting both up, he nodded as if to himself. "Mind if I ask you a question?" he said.

"Fire away," Trench returned.

"Just what the hell were you doing a million miles from nowhere, wandering around with first-degree burns over half your body?" He thought for a moment. "No," he finally said. "Don't answer that. I don't really think I want to know."

Trench laughed. "I couldn't tell you if I wanted," he said. "You see, I don't remember myself."

Body Tech Acquarius' face took on a more serious expression. "I'm not surprised," he said, "after what you've probably been through. Eventually, you may recall everything, or you may not. Only time will tell. The human mind shuts things out, sometimes temporarily, sometimes forever."

"The lady was about to tell me where we are before you came in," Trench said. "Mind if I ask you to finish?"

Body Tech Aquarius shrugged. "Why not?
Basically you're in an abandoned SAC-bomber
command installation twenty miles beneath the
Mojave Desert." He stubbed out his cigaret and
went on. "The place was closed down in 1962 and
probably was off the Soviet nuke priority
targeting programs, so it wasn't hit.

"Our little group took it over two years
before the nukes blew everything to hell. We saw
it coming and made plans. The human race was
bound to fuck everything up and soon. We're the
New People, the rebuilders, the progenitors. We
have one thing the rest of America didn't, a
philosophy. We call it Earthwomb. Earthwomb is
harmony, Earthwomb is balance, the primitive
force of Mother Earthship, and we're all her
children. You, me, everybody."

"You'll meet our First Technician soon," the
blonde girl added. "She'll help you, Death Wings,
she'll—"

"What did you call me?" Trench asked, the
wildness in his eyes making the others step back.
"What was that?"

"Death Wings," she said, pointing to the
tattoo above Trench's heart. "The words 'Death
Wings' were painted on the fired metal found in
the wreckage strewn near where you were
discovered. That is what we have been calling you
throughout the time you hovered near the door to
the Great Unknown."

For the briefest instant, a flicker of
recollection skirted through Trench's numbed
brain. Then it was gone. Somewhere, he had heard
the name before. It had some special significance
to him. But he couldn't remember. Memory was
veiled behind an iron curtain of static.

"You need to rest now," Body Tech Aquarius

said, handing Trench a bottle of pills. "Take two
of these tablets every three hours. They'll help
kill the pain."

They left Trench all alone in the white room
with no windows, many miles beneath the sifting
yellow sands of hell.

15

Artificial light danced on the man-machine's metal flesh.

Surgically interfaced with computerized life-support mechanisms that arrested the mutation process, the internal organs within the biosurvival suit floated in a nutrient soup. If not for the bionic exoskeleton he wore, Luther Enoch would have long since slipped into a Contam state of terminal mutation.

The Dark Messiah stood before an illuminated circular backdrop. The circle contained an interlocking pattern resembling a modified swastika. The elements of the pattern were a triad of interlocking sevens turned on their sides to form a vortex of power.

The number seven had special significance, for a passage in the Book of Revelations attributed six to the Sign of the Beast and seven to the Messiah who would slay the Beast and bring a New Order to mankind.

The symbol was the emblem of the National Church of the Second Coming, the NCSC. Now the official state religion of the United States of

America, the National Church of the Second Coming was a twisted creed which preached nuclear annihilation as the fulfillment of Biblical prophecy, the chaos of a world gone mad as the gateway to Paradise, and genocide as the highest achievement of human energies.

As he stood before the vortex of sevens, the Dark Messiah, Luther Enoch, supreme ruler of the United States of America, the puppetmaster on a global scale who had orchestrated the nuclear exchange which had begun and ended World War III, beheld the products of his evil genius.

And he saw that it was good.

The mesmerized thralls surrounding Enoch's platform wore the masklike expressions of mindless servitude on faces without identity. In the crowd there were no individuals. Only insect sameness.

The sky-blue overalls with the NCSC patch of interlocking sevens on the front and sleeves were worn by women as well as men. Careful selection had chosen only those with superior genetic traits to make up Enoch's inner cadre of elite followers.

The most important of these traits was an inborn drive to obey without question, the innate ability to act without thinking, the primal instinct to suppress the ego and merge with the group mind. All *looked* the same. All *thought* the same. All *were* the same.

Under the influence of LSD 237, Angel Dust, and a variety of potent designer drugs, Enoch's cracked-out puppets rolled around in the deep trance state of a Forward Progression encounter group. Their bodies jerked as hallucinations wracked their nervous systems and the powerful mind-altering drugs they had been dosed with activated hidden neural ganglia in their poisoned brains.

They were in hell.

And loving it.

Their Dark Messiah left the revolving platform in the center of the mass of spasming, gyrating, fit-throwing bodies. His children were now beyond him.

"Have you raised Tallon?" The synthesized voice emerging from the speaker grid in the black steel mask rang with a hollow, metallic sound that sent a thrill of fear racing along the subordinate's spine.

"Yes, Messiah. He's on a scrambled TV patch-through from Las Vegas."

Enoch nodded at his drone. He strode into his situations room, stood before an array of telecommunications screens, and closed the pneumatic doors with the swift manipulation of the console keypad.

There was a faint whir as tiny motors lowered the exoskeleton into the command seat. They were sealed off from electronic eavesdropping, and it was now safe to activate the console bank with the furiously blinking red light atop its central screen.

Tallon's face flashed on the console.

Two thousand miles to the southwest, the merc enforcer stared into the screen of the mobile ADATS strategic-target-designation center, pissing in his camo fatigue pants. Deployed on the tarmac of McCarran Airport just outside Las Vegas, the mobile battle crib was uplinked to an array of orbiting communications satellites.

He didn't look forward to informing Enoch that the man who was the Dark Messiah's only chance at survival—the only known Alpha-Immune in the world—had vanished right off the face of the planet.

Yeah, he thought. Today was definitely not going to be his day.

And, probably, tomorrow wouldn't be either.

The ragged survivors stared in cowed silence as the SCORF hardguys cuffed and shackled the mayor of Helter Skelter, Nevada, and attached his arms and legs to four HUMMER all-terrain vehicles with lengths of high-tensile steel cable.

It was a badguy-tested PLO trick. It was more eloquent than a thousand words. It commanded fear and respect. Mostly fear, but once fear had them by the balls, their respect followed in short order.

Search Team Bandersnatch was under the direct command of the merc named Fast Dancer. Teams Jabberwocky, Shibboleth, Warlord, Draco, and Forbidden Planet were correspondingly under the command of Moebius, Saggitar, Deathlock, Bloodstone, and Quicksilver. All were under the personal direction of John Tallon.

The teams were scouring the shantytowns along the TransAm's escape track with a fine-tooth comb for the Alpha-Immune with a talent for living unlike anything they'd ever witnessed or believed humanly possible.

Fast Dancer signaled the HUMMERS' drivers to put their pedals to the metal. The powerful overhead-cam engines grunted obscenely as the four vehicles sped off in four separate directions, each exerting a force equivalent to 60 times the force of gravity on the body lashed between them.

An earsplitting scream escaped from the victim's mouth as his body was ripped to bloody pieces, leaving only a section of mangled upper torso with the head and the stump of the left arm flailing convulsively on the ground.

The effect had been calculated by Fast Dancer to drive his point home with maximum effect.

Blood spurted in syrupy gouts from multiple wounds as the head crawled on its arm stump before death quieted the wildfiring nerve-endings that jerked the muscles. Body parts attached to the steel cables continued to twitch and spasm, not yet understanding they were dead meat.

From the expressions on the faces in the crowd of scavs, exiles, and Plague victims, Fast Dancer realized he'd driven his point home with a vicious eloquence. After all, a picture *was* worth a thousand words.

"I'm looking for a man," he said addressing the townspeople of Helter Skelter over a bullhorn. "A big man. A man with a tattoo of a bird above his heart. A man known as Phoenix." He paused to let his words sink in.

"There is a bounty of ten thousand n-dollars for any citizen who finds this man. But if we discover that anyone in Helter Skelter is harboring him—well, you've just gotten a taste of our retribution, haven't you?"

A volley of automatic fire dispersed the sullen but intimidated crowd.

The merc spun on the heels of his dust-caked jackboots and strode toward the relative cool of the mayor's office his men had commandeered when they'd roared into the town the day before to begin mass interrogations.

As he was about to leave the execution site, the merc's eye was caught by an attractive woman in the thinning crowd. The woman was with a man and a child. She didn't look like the rest of Helter Skelter's scum people. Before the woman could vanish into one of the rickety buildings of the former ghost town, Fast Dancer hailed her over. Up close the woman was reasonably attractive. Her breasts were fine and high, with long, cylindrical nipples.

Fast Dancer stared into the woman's pale gray eyes and brushed back the long black hair covering half of her face.

As the merc had half expected, there were the festering scars of beta burns on the woman's cheek.

The bitch would do, for lack of anything better. Fast Dancer hadn't had a piece of tail in two days. The merc decided he owed himself some cooze, even if it was scav cooze.

"Blow me," he said, pulling apart the woman's ragged shirt to reveal her large, heavily rounded breasts and whipping out his throbbing erection.

Used by now to obeying orders without question, the woman knelt. The child began bawling and the man began dragging it away.

"No," Fast Dancer said, as the woman took his cock deep into her greedily sucking mouth. "You watch."

The stars glittered over the twisted architectural and human wreckage of Las Vegas like angels having a good laugh at the folly of mankind.

As usual, ultra-pandemonium was the order of the night. You could get any action you needed, if you wanted it bad enough, had the bucks to pay for it, and knew where to go to find it.

The heaviest action was in what was left of Caesar's Palace. Taken over by the Sheik in his post-nuclear power play, the hotel was still the best that Vegas had to offer.

Tonight, the Sheik's Royal Palace was

buzzing with activity. His Imperial Majesty was pulling out all the stops for his honored guest.

"Hookah?" he asked Tallon, profferring an Arabian waterpipe which was filled with a potent mixture of kief, crack, and opium.

"Whatever turns you on," he said as the merc shook his head and instead toked up himself. "Or whatever doesn't, as the case might be."

The Sheik clapped and the first of the night's entertainments came onto the spacious dance floor around which the Sheik's many guests lounged on satin pillows, puffing on water pipes and attended by Vegas's finest prostitutes, wearing see-through harem outfits.

The act was a magician named the Great Monoxide who would saw a woman in half. The novel part of the act—as far as the Sheik was concerned—was that he would use a McCulloch chainsaw and that the woman would never get put back together again.

"My subjects all love me," the Sheik told Tallon as the Great Monoxide revved up his chainsaw and passed it over his screaming subject's naked, tied-down body. "They would do anything for me."

A turbaned waiter hovered nearby, white towel draped across one balloon-sleeved arm while the Sheik's mouthpiece, Shades, nodded at every pearl of wisdom that dropped from his master's lips, the ultimate yes-man.

A thin line of moisture coated the waiter's upper lip. He reached beneath the towel and pulled an icepick from his sleeve.

"*Die, you cur!*" the waiter screamed, lashing out at the Sheik in a savage death-strike.

Without wasting a second, the Sheik shoved the diminutive body of his loyal servant Shades between himself and the lethally jabbing icepick.

The assassin's dagger plunged instead into the royal yes-man's heart.

Two SMG quickbursts from the Sheik's bodyguards disintegrated the waiter's head, leaving behind a stump of spinal cartilage and blood-fountaining arteries.

"Well," said the Sheik as he rolled the punctured cadaver of Shades off him. "*Almost* all of them love me. There are, of course, some anti-social misfits who are ungrateful for the blessings my supreme benevolence bestows upon their miserable personages, but they are few."

The Sheik clapped for a servant to carry the late, lamented Shades away.

"But let us concentrate on other matters, shall we not? You will find this delectable," the Sheik continued as another waiter in desert attire brought out a wheeled table in the center of which was a live prairie dog's head. The small creature was suspended by its head and furiously struggled to escape the trap. The waiter handed steel-headed mallets to the Sheik and Tallon. The Sheik smashed open the prairie dog's skull and began scooping out the brains with a long-handled dessert spoon.

"I'll pass on the appetizer too," Tallon said.

As the Sheik spread some prairie dog brains on a whole-wheat cracker and munched with relish, the Great Monoxide began to perform his feat of surgical legerdemain.

Gunning the screaming buzzsaw, he touched its speed-blurred cutting edge to his screaming subject's midsection. A geyser of blood spewed from the deepening slice in her abdomen as the chainsaw groaned against the thick part of the spinal column before cutting through. The Great Monoxide pointed to the two convulsively shuddering halves of the woman's body with a flourish while the crowd gave him a round of applause.

After the show, the belly dancers came in. Wearing costumes that prominently displayed their breasts and pubic deltas, the dancers performed erotic gyrations using plastic vibrators as props. When the music stopped, the girls circulated freely among the guests.

The party quickly became an orgy in which everybody, including Tallon participated without reservation.

As one of the belly-dancing sluts bucked and thrashed on the merc honcho's face, she made a mental note to inform her contact that the hit had not gone down as planned. Emilio "the Spider" Tarantola would have to try again.

16

"I'm amazed that you're still alive," confessed Elektra-Yang Sunfire, "let alone in one piece. It's hard to believe after the way you looked when one of our work details brought you in."

Trench looked around him. He was in the First Technician's chamber. The large square room had been reached through a network of Earthwomb's miles of subterranean corridors.

"Earthwomb welcomes you, Death Wings."

The diaphanous garment the woman wore revealed two perfectly rounded breasts, tipped by tubular nipples, and the dark triangle of pubic hair between her thighs. Her dark eyes locked with his, capturing his full attention.

Trench let the First Technician of Earthwomb speak, waiting to hear what she had to say. He might as well. A prisoner of his own amnesia, he had nowhere else to go.

"I saw you in a vision, Death Wings," Elektra-Yang went on. "I saw a man who appeared from a blazing funeral pyre. His face was your face and there were dark-feathered pinions surrounding him." She crossed toward him, standing so close he could smell the rich muskiness of her body beneath the diaphanous wrapper, and touched a fingertip to the Phoenix tattoo.

"It was of a bird like this one," the First Technician said. Elektra-Yang smiled. "I wasn't sure if the man was dangerous or benign, a Messianic figure or one capable of terrible annihilation. But I knew the figure was coming. I sensed it."

"And now?" asked Trench. "Are you certain now?"

"No," she returned. "But I intend to find out."

Elektra-Yang let the flimsy wrapper fall to her feet, revealing her naked body. It jutted out in all the right places. She sank to the cushion-littered floor, got on her back, and parted her legs.

"No," she said as she fingered her mink-trimmed sex. "It's not just for my personal pleasure. It's something more. I want to feel your karma. I want to feel it explode inside me. I want to take the measure of its power. I want to sense its heat. Come to me. Now!"

Trench stripped off the white gown he had been given by his attendants after regaining consciousness. The woman's eyes seemed to devour his naked body, focusing on his hardening manhood.

"Put your cock in my mouth," she husked. "I want to taste your essence. Feel it spurt hot and sweet down my throat."

She gently stroked the thick head and the swelling testicles. The shaft throbbed between her lips as she rolled it around in her mouth, purring with satisfaction.

"Now I want you inside me," she said,

breathing deeply. "Yes! That's it!" She gripped his head and pulled him down to her, kissing him deeply. "Don't move!" she gasped. "Just stay there."

They remained locked together for long minutes while a growing buzzing played in Trench's ear. The buzzing grew louder as his pulse rate quickened. Suddenly a blue spark shot across the gap between their heads.

"Now!" she cried. "Fill me!"

Trench moved his hips, rolling and lunging as he plowed her with fierce, long and short strokes. She gasped as he erupted inside her quivering wetness, climaxing simultaneously with him.

"You are the one!" she exulted as she came. "Yes! You are the one!"

Topaz Borealis knelt in the chapel to Mother Earthship. In her prayers she begged that the strange man they had found become healed in body and in mind. Topaz had stayed with him, watching over the Earthling while he tossed and writhed in the grip of nightmarish delusions. She had made a pact with the great Mother Force that he would be hers at the rites of Blast-Off and Re-Entry if he ever awakened.

Topaz prepared for sleep, listening to the pulsating drone of the power generators from deep within Earthwomb's bowels. She likened the generators to Earthwomb's great mechanical heart. The colossal pumps sucking air from the desert above and purifying it of radioactive contaminants were its vast iron lungs. Nestled in Mother Earthship's belly, she would fall asleep without fear.

As she drifted into a contented dream state, Topaz didn't hear the sounds of feet rushing into her compartment. By the time she noticed that she was no longer alone, it was already too late.

The bodies of the deformed, ulcer-covered ghouls reeked of the grave. As they dragged her down the corridors to one of the little-used, pitch-dark feeder tunnels, the ghouls slobbered and gibbered dementedly. Topaz's body was covered with slime as they emerged into a torchlit cavern after many long minutes of navigating the warren of foul-smelling passageways.

There, without saying a word, one of the ghouls hoisted her into the air, impaling her body on an immense hook as though she were a piece of meat. The hook punctured her lungs as it passed through her back and exited under her right breast. Topaz writhed and screamed in mortal agony, but the ghouls paid no attention as she swung from the end of a heavy chain with blood pouring out of her onto the concrete below.

As her pain began to fade with her life in the torchlit cavern, Topaz was able to discern a long line of other bodies suspended from hooks, stretching away for hundreds of feet in either direction. Most seemed to be gutted skeletons from which the flesh and internal organs had been removed. Still alive, others twitched in the final tortured spasms of existence.

Pieces of these bodies were being hacked off by the hideous things that had dragged her down, and devoured while the still-living victims watched helplessly. Topaz closed her eyes, wishing that she would wake up from the terrible nightmare. But inwardly she knew that this was real.

This was happening.

This was a nightmare from which she'd never wake up.

Her last earthly vision was of a jagged scythe of rusted metal, swung by a red-eyed being from hell, that lopped off her head and sent it spinning off into a dark galaxy of eternal nothingness.

Dylan Beethoven was hungry.

He knew it was against the will of the Mother Force to wander the corridors of Earthwomb during his sleep cycle, but Dylan was also a slave to his large stomach. There were soy cakes in the pantry and Dylan Beethoven was going to get some.

The corridors were empty, the only sound was the humming of the overhead flourescents. He pushed open the pantry door and froze in his tracks.

On a table was a human carcass. The carcass had been cleavered open from thorax to sternum. A cluster of repulsive, leprous freaks, chattering like excited chimpanzees, huddled around the corpse, sticking their heads into the raw, open body cavity and coming out with dripping organ parts between their ravenously chomping jaws.

Dylan Beethoven turned to run, realizing he'd inadvertently opened the doorway to destruction, but it was too late. The creatures had already seen him.

Snarling with rage, they left behind the carcass on which they'd been feasting for their new meal. One of the ghouls grabbed Dylan's hand, tearing off his arm at the socket and eating it before Dylan's eyes like a drumstick with fingers. The long bones snapped in the creature's powerfully chomping jaws and it swallowed with a satisfied belch, drinking in the marrow.

The others were tearing him to pieces. One used its long claws to disembowel Dylan with a single furious swipe. His sagging belly sprung open like an overstuffed pillow. A suffocatingly rancid stench emanated from his exposed entrails, which seemed to drive the creatures into a wildly voracious feeding frenzy. His stomach and liver hung briefly by dripping cords of gut tissue before being plucked and eaten like putrescent fruits.

When they had filled their maggoty bellies on Dylan's exposed guts, the slime pack cracked open his skull and scarfed down his brains.

Bliss Body and her lover, Sun Breath, were engaging in forbidden sexual couplings. In a rarely used branch tunnel of Earthwomb they had kept secret from their Monitors, the couple met during the main sleep cycles and performed their illicit acts.

Not until the First Technician signaled the start of Blast-Off the Re-Entry would they be allowed to release their pent-up procreative energies. Until then, they had pledged their bodies and minds to meditation on the great Mother Force.

So absorbed were they in their frantic love game that the stinking, gibbering nightmare things which sprang from the slime-dripping darkness to slice open their bodies, rip out their steaming intestines like links of greasy yellow sausage, and ravenously begin to gorge themselves on their suppurating entrails had no trouble taking their human prey completely by surprise.

All that remained when the gore-dripping hell-spawn shambled back into Earthwomb's depths were the remains of two shattered human skeletons, containing just enough meat for the tunnel rats to pick clean.

"We are preparing for Blast-Off and Re-Entry," declared Elektra-Yang as she and Trench

walked along the corridors of Earthwomb. "This
is a joyous occasion for us. It marks the time
when some of us will leave Earthwomb behind, to
bring our philosophy to the rest of the world."

"From what I'm able to remember of it,
that's like condemning them to death."

"They are ready to die," Elektra-Yang
returned. "Or live. They don't care which. They
have dedicated their souls to Earthwomb. Blast-
Off is pleasure," she went on, "exploding in a
flood of orgasm that lifts their karma off the
launch pad of the earth plane. Re-Entry is the
searing heat of entering the atmosphere. Without
a heat shield, the friction can be murder."

Trench fell silent. All around them, members
of Earthwomb were busily gathering materials to
prepare for Blast-Off. The concrete decks were
being cushioned with soft materials for the ritual
of purification that would impregnate those
children of Mother Earthship who were ready to
conceive. Early conception was an integral
feature of the Earthwombers' philosophy. It
meant there would be more of their number to
spread the sacred teachings and improve the lot
of mankind.

Bundles of sacramental marijuana were
being grown in Earthwomb's vast underground
hydroponics gardens. Housed in rooms whose
walls were highly reflective surfaces and bathed
in hot lights, the plants grew to resinous
succulence. Some of the stash was traded to the
various towns in the area, but most was hoarded
for the use of Earthwomb itself. As grass was its
sacrament, so the potent designer drug SPASM-
X was its opiate. It was prepared in cracking labs
that synthesized the compound from its
component molecules.

A period of celibacy was being observed, to

increase the pleasure and the potency of the sperm which was to be ejaculated into the receiving loins of Earthwomb's female disciples. Masturbation was discouraged for either sex. Meditation and prayer were encouraged instead.

After Blast-Off, Earthwomb's chosen would exit into the nuke-torn world. They would experience the white heat of Re-Entry. Armed with the wisdom of Earthwomb, and a belief in the infallibility of the great Mother Force, they would take their chances in the hostile post-nuclear environment.

"You will be assigned to one of the work crews expanding Earthwomb's dimensions," Elektra-Yang said. She went on to explain that the original shelter was constantly growing. Since the nuclear holocaust, they had increased its area by one third. "We will grow at each Blast-Off. Mother Earthship is kind to us. She sustains us. Protects us. Within the bountiful womb of the Mother Earthship, we have nothing to fear. We are safe, nourished by her, huddling as embryonic masses before the rebirth trauma. Before the purifying heat of Re-Entry."

The darkness stank. It had the putrid stench of a charnel house. Lit by the flickering fires of perdition, the dark, gibbering masses shambling within its fetid embrace paused from their ghoulish banqueting to watch the white-clad figure moving unafraid through their ranks.

The figure passed on, and the unclean things parted like a cloud of bats before a sudden flame to allow it to move freely between them, cowering in fear of its approach.

Coming through the parted sea of slobbering monstrosities from a direction opposite the figure was a subterranean zombie far larger than the rest of his grotesque playmates. The creature's body was covered with pus-dripping sores and cancerous abscesses and many of its organs throbbed obscenely on the outside of its flesh, while its mutated jaws had grown razor-sharp rows of hooked yellow incisors.

Inches from the white-robed figure, it halted, as a nauseating brown gas spurted from the pulsating red gill-slits on the sides of its neck.

"Yes!" the zombie hissed. "The time!"

The creature's member was enormous, crisscrossed by a network of thick, dark veins. An oily yellowish fluid oozed from beneath the head of the erect bluish-purple organ and the network of veins throbbed with anticipation. With a single swipe of its muscular, taloned arms, the ghoul tore away the white robe of the interloper. The shreds fell away revealing the woman's creamy white body. Heavy breasts hung above the narrow waist and flaring hips.

"*Now!*" the First Technician cried, craving the brutal pleasures she knew would follow. "*Begin!*"

Pushing the woman down to her knees, the creature forced his enormous phallus into her mouth. She gagged on the shaft, but swallowed it all, lewdly manipulating her large, erect nipples. Another creature pushed up her ass and inserted his glistening wet rod into her waiting rectal passage.

The three were locked together, pumping each other with debauched savagery while hundreds of dark shapes capered and slobbered in the flickering, torchlit shadows.

Each knew it would have its turn at the woman soon.

Inside her exploding body she could feel the massive phallic members swell as the fluids inside them reached the point of bursting. No sooner had one finished with her than another of the underground uglies emptied its organ into her cunt, anus, face, or breasts.

And then another took the place of the last.

And another, and another . . .

17

The Sheik of Las Vegas awoke one morning several weeks after the Murder Marathon to discover that he was on the verge of taking a long, hard fall.

With SCORF as his kingmaker, Emilio Tarantola's blitzkreig coup to wrest control of Vegas from the Sheik began with a big, ugly bang.

A mechanized column of Commando Ranger light tanks armed with .30-caliber machine guns and LAV 25 light-armored vehicles packing stabilized Hughes M242 Bushmaster 25-mm chain guns, coaxial M240C 7.62-mm machineguns, Mark 19 40-mm grenade launchers, and other lethal weaponry, supported by Bradley M2 IFV tracked vehicles carrying TOW wire-guided missiles and an assortment of HUMMER M998 all-terrain vehicles, sealed off the Casino Triangle between East Sahara Boulevard and Convention Center Drive, effectively isolating the Sheik's Royal Palace.

Anyone who wanted to leave the fire zone before bloody hell broke loose was given exactly three minutes to do so.

Speaking thrugh a public-address system mounted atop the weapons-bristling LAV 25 in which he rode, John Tallon also warned the members of the Sheik's Royal Guardsmen to throw down their weapons and walk toward the SCORF fire positions with their hands above their heads.

A cross-hail of fast-ratcheting autofire from the sandbagged machine-gun emplacements outside the former Caesar's Palace Hotel was the only answer Tallon got. The merc had hoped they'd want to play. He was itching to try out some of the new toys he had. Deadly toys such as the Bradley-mounted TOW missile array, which could deliver a high-explosive warhead with lethal accuracy at extreme range.

A single TOW strike would annihilate anything in a 20-yard radius, instantly turning the Sheik's machine-gun emplacements into funeral pyres for the men who manned them.

At Tallon's fire command, the TOW gunners onboard two of the Bradley M2 IFVs at opposite ends of the isolated strip locked the line of emplacements in the weapon system's laser-guided sights and depressed the large red launch-control button. The gyrostabilized warheads streaked from their turret-mounted firing tubes and struck their targets with pinpoint accuracy.

The only thing left of the Sheik's machine-gun emplacements after the brown cordite smoke cleared were two enormous bomb craters in the street.

Tallon could have easily leveled the Sheik's Royal Palace to its foundations with the heavy firepower from any of a dozen weapons systems at his command, but he had never intended to do so in the first place. The demonstration of the armed might of SCORF had merely been a softening-up tactic. The weapons Tallon would use were not as yet deployed.

Waiting in the squat, black, windowless, and heavily armored military four-by-four called a Commando Ranger were the six lethal weapons Tallon would use to make Emilio the Spider his puppet potentate in Las Vegas after the Sheik's impending fall.

Six men whose combat skills had been honed to the razor edge of action readiness.

A magnificent six who had made a warrior's pact with the Dark Messiah's savage enforcer to bring the man called Phoenix to his knees. Code-named Fast Dancer, Saggitar, Moebius, Deathlock, Quicksilver, and Bloodstone, the merc commandos of Operation Pact of Steel needed one final test of strength before being unleashed on their extremely dangerous quarry.

Now that it was a certainty that the sonofabitch had somehow survived a confrontation with an armed-to-the-teeth F-11 fighter plane, Tallon was especially anxious to avoid any future losses of face in the eyes of Luther Enoch. Search and destroy, *period*, was the name of the game. Nothing less would be good enough this go-round.

Cutting their teeth on the Sheik's stooge army of ex-Mafia buttonmen, cracked-out biker scum, and toilet-paper mercs who'd gotten their asses kicked in Third World firefights from the jungles of El Salvador to the shores of Tripoli would, Tallon figured, give his highly trained but action-starved commandos some hands-on experience in what it would be like to go up against the one-man army called Phoenix.

Against the Phung Hoang, even his commando supermen would need all the help they could get.

Tallon wasn't kidding himself. Phoenix was the best there was. He'd had an eyewitness view of precisely *how* good the Phung Hoang was from the pile of burning radioactive garbage Phoenix had made of SCORF's entire San Francisco operation, destroying it partically single-handedly. The memories of his humiliating defeat still made Tallon grit his teeth in anger.

The surviving defenders of the Royal Palace fell back into the lobby of the mammoth hotel to make a do-or-die stand, expecting SCORF to throw the full might of its take-no-prisoners weapons armory at them in a withering onslaught.

Instead, six lone men in black combat suits strode through the dissipating clouds of high-explosive smoke, as casually as though they were strolling in for a few brews at a Vegas saloon rather than walking straight into the maws of a hundred guns.

Those of the Sheik's merc defenders who tried to score easy takedowns by opening up with saturated machine-gun fire were quickly reduced to bleeding corpses that performed a jerky dance macabre as their targets executed flying pirouettes that put world-class ballet dancers to shame, and tuck-and-roll combos that made any Olympic gymnast they'd ever seen look like they were standing still by comparison.

But these lethal dancers weren't putting on any circus act. Their dazzling choreography was calculated to maximize their killing potential.

Each came out of his precision-executed acrobatic moves clutching flame-belching JATI 9-mm parabellum SMGs and Valmet RPK-78 .30-caliber light machine guns and hurling anti-personnel grenades with a deadly precision more characteristic of mechanized war weapons than of flesh-and-blood human beings.

The six-men housecleaning crew punched through the cordon of dead palace defenders and gained the vast hotel lobby in a few minutes of hard and fast fighting.

Inside the lobby, the members of the SCORF commando unit went into solo action against scores of Royal Guardsmen packing full-auto heat. As each scored fast, clean takedowns and perfect snuffs, they moved toward the pre-designated objective of the operation: the Sheik of Las Vegas's penthouse suite on the top floor of the 60-story hotel.

The Sheik of Vegas might have been called a lot of things in his checkered career, but never dumb.

The self-styled potentate had made certain that there was an emergency escape hatch he could use in case he ever had his balls to the wall.

Not only were the Sheik's nuts up against the woodwork, Tallon was ready to nail them there for good.

That this was the SCORF honcho's handiwork the Sheik had no doubts. He was also fairly certain that the merc enforcer's appointment to the Vegas throne he was being set up to vacate would be the Sheik's Grand Vizier and former Mafia capo, Emilio "the Spider" Tarantola.

The Sheik had no illusions about the fate that awaited him once Tallon's mercs K.O.ed the dwindling opposition and climbed to the Sheik's penthouse suite. Whether it would be a quick and relatively merciful fragburst that would open wet, red places where the sun never shone or a more formal execution after sentencing by a SCORF kangaroo tribunal, the Sheik would wind up just as dead, no matter how you sliced it.

As he threw together as many valuables as he could cram into a large soft-leather Gucci valise and hightailed it to the concealed, private express elevator that would speed him to the car park in the hotel's basement—in which a fast, heavily armored crash-car was parked—the Sheik knew he had one shot and one only.

If he could hole up until after Tallon and the man called Phoenix fought it out and Tallon had pulled out, then Vegas would cease to be important enough to the US-NCSC Government to warrant protecting Tarantola. And the Sheik would then come back again, with a vengeance.

But first he had to get his ass out of the frying pan without getting his privates singed. Even if he could successfully make a break through the escape tunnel that ran underneath the Vegas Strip for six miles and emerged by Freeway 15 on the other side of town, he didn't know what he could do against pursuit by a SCORF Cobra chopper or, worse, an F-11 fighter plane.

All of this became meaningless as the Sheik exited the elevator and was blinded by two halogen-arc headlights. Quickly he heard the turbocharged roar of his fuel-injected Camaro TransAm crash-car screaming down on him on a collision course. Mesmerized with panic, the Sheik threw his arms up and prepared to die as the car advanced to the point where collision was a heartbeat away.

"Need a lift, Kemo Sabe?" called a familiar voice as a head ducked out the window after the Camaro came to a pinpoint stop with its bumper a fraction of an inch away from the Sheik's abdomen.

"Big Wally's air-conditioned limo service to nowhere," the midget went on. "And all it'll cost you, Sheik, is that suitcase you're carrying."

The six-man blitzkreig stood at the apex of a 60-story tower full of lead-bellied corpses and prepared to begin the final phase of their mission.

Splitting up on the penthouse floor, Tallon's merc commandos conducted a methodical room-by-room, putting each potential hiding place through a fine-meshed investigatory sieve until they were certain that the target had fled.

Once Quicksilver and Bloodstone had located the well-concealed elevator shaft situated behind the false wall of a supply closet, it became a highly logical assumption that their target was long gone.

18

Lysergic Moonbase ran her hand along the curvature of her pregnant belly as she prepared herself for Blast-Off and Re-Entry. All Earth-womb was in readiness for the rites of passage into Nukeworld. She had been impregnated at the previous Blast-Off and sensed the embryo developing within her large, round belly.

She looked forward to retiring to the Birth Station deep within Earthwomb's underground bowels, where she and other expectant mothers would await delivery. After giving birth, she would leave Earthwomb, possibly forever. Lysergic Moonbase would be assigned to a place on the nuke-blasted earth where she could help those in need.

This was Re-Entry's essence. *Joypain*; returning home through leaving home.

Her breasts were already swollen with milk, and were tender to the touch as she kneaded them together.

All the prior weeks had been a maze of frenzy, as Earthwomb picked the sweetest reefer from its hydroponic dope gardens and cooked up SPASM-

X in its subterranean crack labs. Lysergic Moon-base's pussy became wet thinking about the effects of SPASM-X on her nervous system. Distributed only during Blast-Off, the psychotropic drug was both an aphrodisiac and a potent hallucinogen. It took you to places unreachable by any other means.

Lysergic Moonbase garlanded her flowing black hair with plastic flowers, lamenting the fact that genuine flowers were far too precious to waste on ornamentation. Only the Monitors merited such perks, and Elektra-Yang Sunfire, the First Technician, and other members of the Select. One day she might be among their number. Now she had to content herself with a plastic gardenia.

Suddenly the raucous klaxons that signaled Thinktank sounded.

It was time!

At last, Blast-Off would begin.

Lysergic Moonbase pressed the stud releasing the pneumatic doors. Locked during sleep cycle, they now opened with a soft hiss of compressed air.

She joined the stream of Earthwomb members, filling the corridors in their flowing white robes, the women with hair garlanded, the men hardly able to contain the sexual excitement they felt at the release from forced celibacy Blast-Off was to bring.

The white-gowned stream flowed toward the Thinktank. Once the operations room of a nuke-missile command center, its dead computer banks and giant tactical screens were still in place, although smashed and rusted beyond repair. As large as a basketball court, the concrete floor of the enormous egg-shaped room was littered along its length with mats for the Earthwombers to recline on throughout Blast-Off.

A circular concrete-and-steel catwalk formed the operations room's upper tier. Here, the Select sat and addressed the disciples of Earthwomb who flowed into the great Thinktank in a human wave, filling it in their childlike innocence.

"We are the embryonic seed of the Mother Earthship! In her protecting womb, we dwell close to her secret heart."

In her flowing robes, with arms upraised, the First Technician of Earthwomb appeared the very image of transcendence over earthly obstacles. Beside the First Technician sat the newcomer whom all knew as her consort.

The man called Death Wings.

The silent one.

The one who worked tirelessly, ceaselessly, and could not remember his past.

"Gog has met Magog on the Plain of Eternity. Great armies have clashed in the Armageddon night before the dawn of Nuke-world. But the Eternal Mothership survives," she continued. "Let us primal to the Mother Force, let us bliss-out on the Earth mandala."

"*Primal to the Mother Force!*" came the surging, responsive chant. "*Bliss-out on the Earth mandala.*"

"*Primal to the Mother Force! Bliss-out on the Earth mandala!* "*Primal to the Mother Force! Bliss-out on the Earth mandala!*"

The First Technician of Earthwomb looked down at her flock. She smiled in benediction. Her face radiated a transcendental serenity, as if she had seen the future and it was as filled with promise as the present was littered with the maggot-blown corpses of the dead.

Silence descended on Thinktank as it awaited

the First Technician's coming words. She played to the silence, beginning when their expectance was at its peak.

"Corrupters have engulfed the planet in nuclear hellfire," she said, her voice ringing out over the massed love children at her feet. "They have defiled Mother Earthship with the radioactive excrement of their loins.

"Now it is up to us to purify the loins of the Mother. We must go forth and make Nukeworld live again. Make it once again what it had been in the Eden-times before man trod the ground and spat upon it in his debased greed and his unholy blindness."

She awaited the silence following the impassioned chants of "Primal to the Mother Force!" and "Bliss-out on the Earth mandala!" from her enthralled audience.

"Today," she went on, "those of you in which the seed of life has taken root will go forth into a new beginning. You will know the joy of birth, after which you will be sent out into Nukeworld.

"Men of the Age of Blast-Off and Re-Entry and women who have not as yet conceived but have nevertheless reached the Age will also be sent forth into Nukeworld.

"Earthwomb's colonies are everywhere. Beneath the planet's crust. In cool, fertile valleys. On the barren peaks of remote mountaintops. Even in the ruins of the nuked cities, we exist, to bring about the rebirth of the poisoned world, the repurification of the noxious environment."

Robed figures with eyes that did not have the blank look of Earthwomb's disciples circulated amid their ranks. They were of the Select, and they carried bowls containing yellow capsules. They were capsules of SPASM-X.

The Earthwombers solemnly took the

capsules, popped them into their mouths, and swallowed. Soon they would feel the magic which SPASM-X released. Soon they would become as gods, their reward for assuming the burden of raising humanity up from its own ashes. Soon SPASM-X would send them into the heaven they had only dreamed about these long months.

"Let the power of the Earth Mother enter you through SPASM-X," intoned the First Technician as the drug began taking effect. "Let SPASM-X transport you. Let SPASM-X mutate your brain and send your soul into another dimension. You are becoming antimatter. Light as starshine, you will float. Raise yourselves . . . become as gods. After all, you deserve a break today."

SPASM-X stimulated the sexual centers in the hypothalamus. Its powerful hallucinogenic mixture enhanced both the production of sperm and the fertility of the egg in the womb.

It acted almost instantly.

Its effects lasted six hours, then dropped off sharply.

All over Thinktank's vast space, the Earth children were shucking their white robes. Flawless naked bodies gleamed under the lights as they began coupling, while the drugbearers looked on and smiled their benedictions.

Lysergic Moonbase eagerly accepted the hard cocks which sought to probe her mouth and cunt. She knelt on all fours and rapturously sucked three hard organs at once, while another pair penetrated her cunt and asshole. As soon as the hot semen spurted, more took their place. She drank down all she could, and still was thirsty for more.

The Thinktank quickly became a mass of writhing human bodies. Cocks pistoned into cunts with the speed of sexual fury. Under the influence of SPASM-X, the celebrants changed partners with amazing speed, unable to withstand the urge to copulate.

"Awesome," Elektra-Yang said to Trench as she and others of the Select sat on their parapet and watched the writhing human sex pit below.

"When is it our turn?" asked Trench.

"We don't get a turn. The stuff isn't meant for us," she answered him.

"Why not?"

"You don't really want to know," she responded. The First Technician turned back to watching the orgiastic couplings below. A fierce brilliance burned in her eyes as though she were gazing into the heart of the sun.

"Have some of this instead," she said. She passed Trench a think joint of hydroponic pot.

The orgy continued until it reached the limits of physical endurance. There was simply a point beyond which the body could no longer function.

The intoxicated celebrants lost interest as narcosis set in. They became catatonic as fatigue took over and SPASM-X was metabolized by the body.

The Monitors now led them out of Thinktank.

"Blast-Off is a definite go. Prepare for Nukeworld Re-Entry," they whispered softly as the Earth children they selected obediently followed. Hand-held indicators which the circulating Monitors carried flashed when in proximity to a microscopic subcutaneous implant in those of the Age of Blast-Off.

Lysergic Moonbase exploded as the last of several hundred orgasms rocked her from head to toe. Her last in a long succession of lovers pulled out his erect phallus and lay back on soft

cushions. Lighting a joint he toked leisurely, and
drifted away into visions of inner bliss.

She felt a hand grasping her arm.

"It is time," a well-modulated voice told her.
"Time to go to the Birth Station. To have your
child. To prepare for Re-Entry." She looked up
into the face of a Select. The face wore a beatific
smile. "Nukeworld awaits you, my child."

Lysergic Moonbase was filled with an inner
bliss that suffused her entire being. At last, she
would experience the joypain of Re-Entry. Naked,
she rose and allowed the Select to lead her to the
Thinktank's exitway, joining a queue of other
naked, pregnant women.

Offhandedly, she noticed that men, as well as
women who did not seem to be pregnant, were
being escorted from the Thinktank through
separate exits. When she asked the Monitor why
this was, she was told that a great revelation
awaited her and that she must be patient.

A bank of freight elevators brought her and
scores of other pregnant women to a sublevel
deep within the poured-concrete bowels of the
complex.

There were roughly two hundred other
pregnant Earth children beside herself in a vast
underground vault, its concrete ceiling supported
by rows of massive concrete pillars, stained with
rust from seepage from underground springs.
Naked bulbs strung at intervals from the
decaying ceiling cast a dim, shadowy glow in the
tomblike space. The air reeked of damp stone and
the decaying corpses of the giant mutant rats
that lived down there. Pools of oily black water
had turned sections of the floor into miniature
lakes and dripping stalactites and stalagmites
hung from the concrete ceiling and grew from its
floor like the immense glass teeth of a giant's

jaws.

All the women were naked like herself. Under the effects of SPASM-X and hours of constant orgasms they were docile and in a state of deep narcosis. They sprawled in a state of twilight sleep, awaiting the next phase of their journey.

None of them realized it was a journey into death.

Dark figures suddenly materalized from gaping ruptures where sections of the concrete walls had collapsed, gibbering and slavering as their slitted red eyes sighted their prey.

It was feeding time in hell.

The slobbering scum things grabbed the pregnant women and dragged them down into the dark, stinking rabbit-warren of tunnels that spread from the vault, not caring how they got them into the deepest sublevels of Earthwomb which they inhabited like obscene things at the lightless bottom of the sea.

Lysergic Moonbase screamed as a scaly black hand tipped with razor-edged claws grabbed her by the breasts and savagely ripped them off. She screamed, but a second swipe of the claws tore the vocal cords from her larynx. They hung in bloody strips from the gushing cavity in her throat. The creature dragged her by her long hair while her mutilated voicebox refused to translate the scream in her brain into sound.

Others were raped right on the spot. The phallic members of their new lovers caused them to howl in agony. The immense organs were too large for human openings. The shafts lacerated internal organs as they were brutally rammed in. The highly acidic fluids spurting from them liquified flesh on contact.

Some of the sublevel scum ghouls couldn't

contain themselves. They had been waiting too long.

Gripping their prey by the legs, they used their fanged incisors to tear away the vagina, ripping the pubic hair and the flesh beneath it like nauseating body scalps to expose the fetuses within. Wet with amniotic fluids, the embryos were pulled violently from the wombs of their mothers. Trailing umbilical cords and placental sacs, they were torn apart in a feeding frenzy before their mothers' eyes.

Those who were dragged down into the dark, acrid-smelling feeder tunnels were hung from meathooks jabbed through the throat, stomach, chest cavity, or groin. As the life spurted from their ruptured bodies, they watched their sisters being hacked open and the succulent young being broiled alive by flaming torches and devoured by the hideous creatures that inhabited Earth-womb's bowels.

In the moldering, poured-concrete, steel-reinforced womb of Mother Earthship, a fatal parasite had taken occupancy.

The Grim Reaper was its name.

Its black harvest was the stuff that dreams are made of.

In the diseased belly of Mother Earthship, all systems were go.

19

The Thinktank was emptying out.

The revelry had subsided.

Another Blast-Off had been successfully brought to its final stage.

The Select smiled knowingly at one another.

Continuance of Earthwomb had been assured for another cycle.

Trench wondered what purpose the orgy could serve. To him, it was just another blue movie.

"Did it inspire you?" Elektra-Yang asked.

"Yeah," said Trench. "It was almost a religious experience."

The First Technician of Earthwomb smiled enigmatically.

"Come," she told him. "I have a surprise for you."

Clasping Trench's hand in hers, she led him from the Thinktank through a network of aseptic white corridors. Their destination was a room far from the Thinktank zone.

"What's the surprise?" Trench asked.

"In a little while you'll see," she said

beaming.

Seconds later, Trench saw what the surprise was. It wasn't the best one he'd ever had, though.

Five men were pointing automatic weapons at him. The one in the center held a CAM portable unit, programmed for Plague lentivirus Immune response. The CAM's LED readouts were going haywire. It was in the proximity of two Immunes: Trench and the woman who quickly moved out of their automatic weapons' line of fire.

"These gentlemen are your escorts to hell," Earthwomb's First Technician explained. She still wore the beaming smile. Trench realized the lady was sick. As in mentally sick.

"What the hell's going on?" he protested.

"You had to remember who you were sooner or later," she responded. "When that happened, I realized the party would be over. So you have to go now, lover boy. Before it's too late. And since you have to go I might as well profit by it."

She saw the puzzled look on Trench's face and continued. "These gentlemen are bounty hunters, lover boy. They sell Immunes to the Government. You're an Immune with a big price on your head. You're worth ten grand in gold. I get a sixty-forty split, my way."

"What about those high-sounding philosophies you've been spouting?"

"Just another way to turn a buck. You see, this place used to be a top-secret research facility called Gryphon. It was part of the MX missile complexes that honeycomb this part of Nevada—nearly five thousand dense-packed silos buried under millions of tons of reinforced concrete. We were involved in a project to clone human beings for the military, had been since the early seventies. Our biggest problem was getting them to breed true. All known human clones to date had been infertile.

"Then my husband came up with a brilliant solution. A drug called SPASM-X. It made the clones fuck like bunnies. At the same time, it assured an over ninety-five-percent fertility rate.

"Enter the nukes, and fifteen years of hard work all came to an end. Like most of the staff, my husband caught the Russian Plague virus and mutated into a Contam. I was lucky. I was immune to the effects of Plague. Those of us who remained human had to isoalte off the Contams our friends and family members had become for our own protection. Nevertheless, we still felt a responsibility to take care of them. And we continue to do so, in our own ways. . . ."

Her voice fell off and a hard light came into her ice-blue eyes.

"Blast-Off and Re-entry," Trench said.

"Precisely," Elektra-Yang Sunfire replied. "Like Confucius, I've reduced my entire philosophy of life to one basic precept."

"That wouldn't be 'When in doubt, punt,' by any chance, would it?"

"Not even close," she said. "It goes like this: 'Watch out for Number One—step on all the other numbers.' "

"Now get him the fuck out of here," she screamed.

At that moment, Trench remembered the faces in the dream. They were the faces of his family. He remembered the megadeaths in San Francisco and Jake Hassler, September Song, and the other members of the Nuclear Family in the ruins of the TransAmerica Tower. He recalled John Tallon, the merc out to nail his ass. He remembered the Murder Marathon in Vegas and the escape from Tallon's SCORF hit team. He remembered the blinding flash of the heat-

seeking STINGER missile detonating, bathing
him with hellfire. . . .

And he put the rest together.

All in a flash.

"All right, Twinkie," said the lead bounty
hunter. "The party's over. Say goodbye to the
lady and shake your shit."

Trench wasn't about to argue with the heavy
metal these bozos were carrying. They were
punks, true. But they were hardcase punks who
wouldn't hesitate to splatter his innards all over
the walls if he made the wrong move at the wrong
time. He knew he was worth as much to them
dead as he was alive. More importantly, they
were the kind of badmen who didn't care much
which.

"See you in hell," Elektra-Yang called out.

"Send me a postcard," Trench returned.

The bounty hunters filed out into the sterile
corridor. Ahead, a branch tunnel sheared off at a
perpendicular angle. They'd use the freight
elevator at the corridor's end to bring him
topside, where their backups were probably
deployed. The time to act was now. Shaking them
now, Trench could easily lose the bounty hunters
in the dark sublevels where tracking him would
be harder than finding a needle in a haystack. The
hunters had made a major mistake. They'd tied
his hands . . . but they'd neglected to do the same
to his feet.

Whirling to deliver a double thrust-kick
combo, Phoenix disarmed the hunter immediately
behind him. The hard edge of his sandaled foot
slammed into the bad dude's side, fracturing the
short bones of the ribcage and sending a hail of
jagged bone splinters into the ugly's liver and
stomach. The badass belched blood and
staggered into his hard pard.

A domino effect bowled over the rest of the

rat pack like a line of targets in a shooting gallery. But it didn't look like Trench could make the side corridor before their SMGs drew a bead on his back. Feeling time crawl past, he made a desperate dash for the corridor. When he heard the bolts click home on the hunters' subguns, Phoenix knew it was too late. Before he could even hear the shot, he'd feel the scorching death agony as molten 9-mm slag razored his heart and scrambled his brains. . . .

"Down!"

Autofire chattered as Trench hit the deck, narrowly avoiding a brace of 7.56-mm flesh-shredders that whizzed overhead from the chattering Steyr AUG .223 submachine gun. The lethal spray caught the hardguys behind Trench like a nest of roaches in a poison mist. Only this mist was made of fast-cycling lead. They threw up their hands and did the terminal watusi, leaking their fluids as the jerking corpses sucked the floor.

A knife gleamed in the little man's hand. Big Wally cut the ropes binding Trench's wrists.

"Out of the niiiight, when the full moon is bright, comes the horseman known as Zorro," he sang as he sawed. *"This bollld renegade carves a zeee with his blaaaade. . . .*

"That's another one you owe me," the midget said as Phoenix's bonds snapped. "Looks like you're helpless by yourself, Trench."

"What happened to the eye patch, runt?" Phoenix asked, noticing Big Wally now seemed to have two perfectly good eyes.

"That's 'the world's *tallest* runt' to you," Big Wally answered. "Lost it in a crap game."

Some of the hunters' weapons were still functional. Trench checked the action on a JATI SMG that had been blown from the grasp of one with the hand still clutching it. He separated the severed hand and snapped the breach bolt. A parabellum round clicked crisply into the subgun's chamber.

"The rescue act. Why?" he asked, trading his robes for a dead hunter's clothes.

"The answer's simple," Big Wally replied. "Nevada used to be a fun state till you turned up. The sooner you split, the better."

Trench glowered at the little guy. He picked him up by the legs and dangled Big Wally upside down.

"Run that by me again," he said.

"Okay, okay," Big Wally answered. "So the Sheik paid me to track you down. He figured you were his best bet at getting his ass back on the throne." Big Wally gave Phoenix a quick rundown on the coup that had deposed the Sheik in favor of Tallon's puppet potentate.

"Every cactus farmer in these parts knows where the Government put access ports to the MX system," continued the little man. "It was only a matter of doing a little barging around in the dark before I turned you up."

The sound of booted feet echoing on concrete caught their attention.

"Here comes the cavalry," Big Wally said. "Which way is up?"

"I figured you'd be able to tell me that," Trench said, "seeing as you got yourself down here."

Big Wally shook his head. "Getting down here and getting back up again," he said, "are two different things. This place is a five-hundred-mile maze, Trench."

Trench looked down the length of the dark access corridor. "Then I guess that makes us rats, doesn't it?" The debris-strewn concrete tunnel snaked down into the black depths of Earthwomb.

20

Déjà vu was the only word to describe it.

Phoenix had the all-too-familiar feeling of having been here before. Down in the nightworld. Deep in the moldering concrete catacombs that men, like technological moles, had tunneled in the earth to shelter themselves from the mega-tonnage they feared from the skies.

When had America become a nation honey-combed with secret underground installations hidden in its bedrock like pockets of disease in the vitals of a terminal patient?

When had the makers of the bombs, the cookers of the biochemical agents, the toyers with the stuff of the DNA chain first begun their wormlike excavations into the planet's guts?

It didn't matter. They had been digging in for decades, as though realizing that one day, in a hellfire flash of nuclear apocalypse, they would be hurled back to the caves from which their race had taken ten million years to crawl toward the technological mastery of the earth.

In this nuclear Stone Age, the shattered survivors repopulated the underground

complexes which had either been abandoned by
the God-players or become their tombs. They
scurried   among   the   smashed   temples   of
Olympian technology, using what they still
possessed the knowledge to use, and leaving the
rest to the mutants and the maggots and the rats.

Earthwomb was such a place. Deep in its
plundered concrete shrines to the fiery gods of
nuclear destruction, it had all the right elements
for the noxious progeny of biochemically induced
Plague to breed and develop into the nightmarish
spawn of terminal madness.

Emerging from a dark flight of concrete
stairs, Trench and Big Wally found themselves in
a cavernous sublevel. Either it had been
abandoned earlier than the upper portions of the
devastated MX missile complex or it had never
been fully completed.

Concrete corridors covered with stone-eating
fungal growths, and showing the rusted brown
grids of their steel reinforcements where sections
had fallen away, trailed off into eerie darkness.

Electrical cables and power conduits dangled
uselessly from the ceilings like the severed
arteries of some enormous beast, although from
hidden generator sources—probably the same
ones that powered the upper levels—there came
enough power to keep a few bulbs dimly lit.

The corridor stank of animal excrement and
other putrid odors. The stench of rotting corpses
was everywhere. It came from the carcasses of
things that had died in the unlit depths.

The stench lessened as the tunnel took them
into a larger vault that looked as though it had
once been an operations center of some sort.
Emplacements for banks of computer terminals
stood at odd points in the huge chamber,
although most of the equipment had been

stripped from the steel framework.

Falling debris had partially blocked the mouth of the access corridor leading from the chamber. Straining to push aside heaps of metal wreckage and concrete debris, Trench and Big Wally entered the dark subterranean passageway.

They didn't see the reflective yellow eyes tracking them as they advanced down the corridor.

Attacking quickly, the scum ghouls dropped from huge ventilation ducts in the ceiling and leaped from great holes in the floor like profane jack-in-the-boxes. The scores of shambling obscenities seemed to materialize out of the shadows of the corridor themselves.

"Hell's bells!" Big Wally sang out. There was no mistaking the goon crew of attacking uglies, even in the dim light.

"Contams!"

Two enormous Plague-spawned goblins lunged simultaneously at Trench. They wielded pieces of machinery converted into crude metal pikes studded with razor-edged cutting surfaces. The Contams' lips skinned back from hooked yellow fangs. Festering tumorous masses covered their deformed bodies. The musculature of each was visible on the outside, rippling and flexing powerfully as they went into their death swings.

Sidestepping quickly, Trench evaded the lethal harpoons, countering with a flying Drunk Monkey roundhouse-fist combo that shattered the first Contam's skull like an overripe melon. On the follow-through, he caught the second Contam with a 9-mm JATI SMG burst, coming up in perfect synchronization from a sideways roll that had brought him up behind the second hellfiend.

A high-velocity fragburst caught the Contam just below the neckline as he raised the lethal steel club overhead to gain momentum for a headbuster swing. The combined force of the bullets and the backward momentum of its arm toppled the Contam backward.

It fell hard on the bristling mass of razor projections of its own weapon, impaling itself. Greenish blood glistened on the tips of barbed metal spikes that punched through the Contam's abdomen.

Big Wally had eluded another Contam death duo which had tried to corner the little guy. Getting between their legs, the midget thought fast and acted faster. Unhooking two grenades from his utility belt, he pulled the cotter pins with his teeth and pitched each lethal antipersonnel device underhand. The steel pineapples slid along the tunnel floor like shuffleboard disks, detonating with two powerful, fiery concussions a split-second apart between each Contam's legs.

Ragged chunks of charbroiled mutant body parts stuck to the walls as the Contams left this mortal coil. A mass of beating organ tissue splattered the midget as he dove for cover, a heartbeat ahead of the blast.

He held up his hand and flashed Trench the thumbs-up signal.

Trench and the little guy braced for a second wave of Contam attackers. Stock still, they hunkered in the shadows, but nothing happened.

"It could be that's all there is," ventured Big Wally. "Just a small group of scavengers."

"Or it could be we just woke a couple from their sleep cycle," Trench countered. "The way these things breed, it's even money there's scores, maybe hundreds more down here."

"Didn't I see a fire exit back there?"

"That's just what we're looking for," returned Trench, unamused by Big Wally's remark. "Come on, runt. We've got our work cut out for us."

Trench and Big Wally picked their way carefully down a feeder corridor, cursing the shadows and the cold, oily liquid that ran along its floor. Attack could come from any of a dozen different directions or every direction at once, and they'd barely have a second to see it coming.

They'd know when the strike went down only when the Contams were practically on top of them. Without a map of the installation, there was no way to be certain that an alternate route topside even existed.

Coming to a spot in the sprawling network of feeder tunnels where the concrete arteries branched in two directions, they decided to take the right fork. The left didn't feel right; it was too dark and the air smelled rank with rot. On the other hand, the right seemed to have the slightest trace of circulating airflow. As they moved along it, they could feel the circulating currents become stronger.

"Hey, looks like we're—"

"Shut up!" Trench hissed through clenched teeth.

He'd just heard voices. Human voices.

They came from just up ahead.

Inching softly toward the end of the corridor, Trench and Big Wally found themselves on the brink of a deep concrete pit.

Once a metal catwalk-and-ladder system had connected their corridor with the pit below, which had probably housed generators or other heavy equipment or a workshop or research lab. Now, the steel superstructure lay mostly in pieces on the floor of the circular concrete pit. Only a steel gantry, running along the high ceiling from which a heavy-duty winch hung, remained.

The generator the pit now housed was of a more primitive variety. One that ran on human power. Around a huge metal turnstile obviously cannibalized from the fallen catwalk, young men in the rags that had once been the flowing white robes of Earthwomb's children struggled to turn the mammoth crank.

Contams stood guard, wielding clubs and other makeshift weapons. Most of the Contams wore the ragged remnants of military uniforms and technicians' coveralls.

As Trench and Big Wally looked down, one of the clones staggered and fell out of step. A Contam overseer in a torn uniform with Captain's hashmarks stalked over and delivered a crushing blow to the spine. The broken body was hurled into a huge trough of corrosive chemicals.

The clone's death screams were drowned out by the hiss of the powerful acids that consumed his body. A replacement clone was quickly brought in to take the corpse's position in the chain gang.

"Heartbreaking, ain't it," Big Wally commented. "Well, I guess we'll just have to backtrack and see if we can find us another way outta here—"

"We're going down, runt," Trench shot back.

"Down!" the midget returned as loud as he could without giving away their positions. "You kidding or what? In case you haven't noticed, the only way down is feet-first, and brother, that first step is a real doozie. And furthermore, with the couple odd rounds we got left we might as well go in sticking out our index fingers and shouting, 'Bang, you're dead.'"

"You're wrong on both counts," Phoenix

answered. "I'm going down. You'll cover me. And the only way out is through those clones. Chances are one of them knows an exit. Earthwomb has surface operations too. The clones are used to farm and scavenge."

Handing Big Wally his JATI SMG, Trench went back into the tunnel, dragging one of the immense wooden storage spools of coaxial cable he'd noticed piled some ways back toward the tunnel's mouth. His muscles screamed as he cast the cable and snagged the big steel hook of the gantry winch on the first try.

Hoping the noise from the pit would continue to mask his play, Phoenix pulled the lassoed winch toward him. He estimated there was enough cable to get him down on a shallow swing.

Big Wally got into position with the Steyr AUG, laying the JATI SMG on the floor. The Austrian-made, full-auto, advanced-technology assault weapon had better controllability and longer range than the JATI, which was chambered for .45 ACP ammos as opposed to the 7.62-mm NATO frag rounds the AUG fired. Furthermore, he still had a full 40-round clip in the AUG while there were only a few rounds left in the JATI.

"Okay," the midget said, handing Phoenix his SMG. "Go for it, pard."

Slinging the JATI over his shoulder and locking his hands around the humongous iron hook, Trench pushed away from the edge of the hanging corridor using every ounce of strength in his heavily muscled thighs and calves. The tension of the heavy rubber-jacketed coaxial cable helped add momentum to his swing.

The Contams were alerted to the overhead movement as the invader flew through the air. But for one of them it was already too late.

Phoenix rode the swing well past the bottom of its counterclockwise arc to build momentum and let go at the top of the backswing, simultaneously doing a full body twist to put his face toward the targets.

Two booted feet landed hard enough to crush the bones of the Contam's skull with a sharp, cracking sound. Internal pressure caused the slitted yellow eyes to pop from their sockets. Two streams of bloody foam mixed with chunks of spurting brain matter as the Contam kissed a world he'd never made a short goodbye.

A three-round fragburst from the JATI reduced a Contam scum ghoul who was coming at Trench from behind, swinging a mean-looking sonofabitch of a club, to a headless corpse, pitching wildly on two legs without a brain to guide them.

The arm and the club sailed through space, burying the weapon's spiked head in the chest cavity of one of the captive clone slaves and splitting open the innocent bystander who had been unlucky enough to get caught in the cross fire. But innocents sometimes died in a firefight. This one was no exception.

Two Contam heads got bashed together as a round of savage Laughing Crane knife-slash hands made mush out of their pulmonary cavities. Blood and urine burst from punctured organ bags, spurting poison through the crippled mutants' systems. The critically injured monstrosities sagged to the concrete floor, retched, and fell down dead.

Another JATI quickburst took out a Contam scuzz crew which was coming up through a large hole in the pit. They quickly became dead little pieces of mangled mutant. Trench signaled to Big Wally and the little man threw him a grenade. To make sure they'd have no more mutant play-mates, Phoenix pulled the pin and dropped the grenade into the hole. The resulting explosion was music to his ears.

"Okay," he said to the clones after the dust settled. "Who wants to live?"

21

"We have nothing to lose by helping you but our shackles," the clone leader told Trench. The clone's face was a mass of scars from countless beatings. "Earthwomb promised us freedom. Instead, they gave us death."

"You know of a way out of here?" Trench asked.

"Yes!" another of the formerly enslaved clones spoke up. "I know a way. The evil ones made me work on the surface for a long time. The place is not far."

Trench called Big Wally to come down. The midget shimmied along the black cable to the floor of the pit with surprising agility and speed.

"Always got an A in gym," he said, shoving a cigar into his mouth and lighting it.

Altogether, there were eleven men moving through the silent corridors beneath the former MX missile-silo complex stretching for miles beneath the desert above. The clone who knew the way out led the group, accompanied by Phoenix holding the JATI at hip level ready for instant cover fire. Big Wally brought up the rear as the end point, waving the Steyr AUG back and forth like a divining rod for danger.

Backtracking from the pit through the tunnel from which they had come, the clone guide veered into a gap in the wall feeding into a network of maintenance alcoves and access tunnels that led to a sublevel which had not been plundered the way the preceding section had.

This area appeared to have remained functional right up to the end, surviving the first strategic nuke strike only to be wiped out by Soviet biologicals.

Although doors had been blown off their hinges, and the offices beyond strewn with over-turned furniture and littered with heaps of documents, the rooms lining the dimly lit corridor were more or less intact.

At the consoles of radar screens and computers, human remains were sprawled in a variety of positions signifying gruesome deaths.

Many were mummified. Others were little more than skeletons with the rags of military uniforms clinging to the crumbling, half-eaten remains as grim testaments to the folly of mankind's overweening pride. It was a folly known to the ancient Greeks, who called it hubris—the pride that offends the gods and brings their awesome retribution.

Man always loses at the game of playing God.

This time he'd lost big. And probably for good.

The MX complex's battle stations were still manned by an army of cadavers. They had died instantly when lethal CBW toxins inundated the ventilation ducts. Biological agents too small for even the most sophisticated filters to screen out and too toxic for any antidote to counter in time had killed them where they sat.

Before the remains of the greatest technology the world had ever known lay the decaying remains of those who had built and manned the mechanisms of global annihilation.

They'd tried to play God, only to become maggot food.

But Trench wasn't in the mood for meditating on the folly of man. Justice was justice. And contrary to accepted convention, *poetic* was one thing it never was.

Brutal, yes. Ugly, yes. Often hideously so. But poetic? No fucking way.

Still, from these grim signs of recent occupation, Trench caught a glimmer of hope that something very precious to his own immediate chances of survival might be close at hand.

For whatever reasons—maybe a lingering memory in their mutant brains of the men they had once been—the Contam grave robbers had left this section largely unmolested.

In the nerve center of an underground battle crib like this one, the security station couldn't be far. That meant weapons caches. If they were still intact, more than the JATI SMG with an almost empty magazine he held in his hand would soon be available.

Trench had the uneasy but nevertheless all-too-distinct feeling that when they hit topside the shit would begin to fly in earnest. They were going to need all the firepower they could carry.

Wishing he had a starlight scope to cut through the blackness, Trench strained his vision for signs of what he knew could be close at hand yet easily overlooked in the twilight of the tunnel. As the group moved around a bend in the corridor, he suddenly found what he'd been looking for—an ordnance supply room.

"Don't move," Trench told the lead clone, holding him back with an arm across his emaciated chest. He signaled to Big Wally to come over with a wave of his hand.

"Tell me you have some plastique," he said.

"Okay," returned Big Wally. "I have some plastique."

"Now give it to me."

"I can't," Big Wally said. "I don't have it."

"I told you not to tell me that," Trench said. Big Wally shrugged and unclipped a grenade. It would have to do.

Trench threw the pineapple and dove for cover. The explosion of the grenade could bring trouble in the form of another Contam assault wave, whereas the plastique's force could be shaped for minimal noise. Crude though it may have been, the grenade was effective. The steel-plate door of the weapons room splintered like matchwood under the impact of the blast. A single kick of Trench's booted foot was enough to tear it right off its hinges.

Paydirt!

Racks in the room's center held enough firepower to fight a small war. A quick glance showed M161A1s, MACs, and other SMGs and the big machine guns, several EM3 carbine versions of the M-60, and a couple of advanced technology AMELLI M9GV Squad MGs. And yeah, there was a standard-version MINIMI M249.

Plenty of ammo was there for the grabbing on heavy-duty steel racks against three of the supply room's walls, as well as grenades and other ordnance. The deadly accessories included C-5 plastique explosive, exploding rocket heads capable of being launched from any of the automatic weapons in the room, claymore mines,

and wooden crates containing thousands of fully
loaded 32-round magazines.

Trench and Big Wally stocked up on the
deadly goodies while the clones looked on. Trench
caught one of them playing with a .45 ACP Sig-
Saur autopistol.

"Put that down," he said. "That's a weapon,
not a toy."

"These kill, yes?" asked the clone leader.
"They take the lives of those to whom they point.
Is this correct?"

"Yeah, they sure do," Trench returned.

"Then give us these weapons. We want to kill
those who have oppressed us." A murmur of
assent rose from the group of clones. Trench read
in their eyes an emotion that made them all too
human: hatred. They minds had been like blank
computer disks ready for programming. Now
hatred had been imprinted into their memory
banks. It would be part of the program from now
on.

Putting heavy metal into these guys' hands
would be like giving out TNT to pre-schoolers.
They'd only hurt themselves. On the flipside,
there was no way they were going to live more
than a few more hours anyway, absolute max.

No sense kidding yourself, Phoenix thought.
Once they got topside they'd be early casualties.
Trench was just using them to get himself and
Big Wally to safety and he knew it. The clones
were as good as dead one way or the other.
Phoenix decided he might as well let the clones go
out like something they'd never been throughout
their perversely brief existences: men.

He handed each clone an M161A assault rifle
and extra ammo clips.

"How are these weapons operated?" asked
the head clone.

"Just point it and shoot," Big Wally answered. He snapped a fresh 7.62-mm clip into the Steyr AUG and shouldered the pack he'd filled with heavy armaments and ordnance.

Loaded down with weapons, they exited the munitions room. A shaped plastique charge insured that the room would never supply anyone with firearms again. Big Wally stuck the timer into the soft claylike mass of C-5 explosive and depressed the arming button. Ten seconds later, there was the deafening explosion as the room went up in a ball of flame that sluiced in a flood of orange fire through the corridors beyond.

The guide clone led the group toward a shaftway that angled down into the darkness. For a few hundred feet they followed it down, then crossed a narrow steel walkway across a ventilation shaft with a seemingly bottomless drop, toward another corridor. This one contained a concrete stairwell which the clone guide claimed led to the surface.

It took the better part of an hour, with two rest stops for Big Wally and the clones, before reaching an atmosphere interlock at the surface level of the MX complex.

The huge steel door was bolted shut.

Big Wally shaped another charge of C-5 plastique around the tumbler device, jammed in a timer, and stepped back. The massive concussive force of the high explosive was effectively focused on a small area, driven outward by the configuration of the ordnance. Little of the force went anywhere else. Most of the three-inch-thick high-tensile steel door disintegrated like blow-torched tinfoil. The remains hanging from the frame flapped in the hot desert wind.

Sunlight streamed in. The intense rush of

heat confirmed that they had come up in the middle of the afternoon.

Trench edged close against the door frame. Nudging the remainder of the door open with the muzzle of his MINIMI MG, he peered outside. A blacktop parking area, its hurricane fence smashed and military vehicles overturned and rusting to junk, lay between him and the parched Mojave desertscape.

Blown by the wind, the desert sand had already begun to swallow up the installation. Beneath a sky so vibrantly blue it hurt to look at it after months in the colorless monotony of Earthwomb, the desertscape stretched northward to distant sandstone bluffs. Heat shimmers made the mountains appear like hellish giants brooding over the prehistoric death-grounds.

A black line of highway stretched east and west, paralleling the line of wrinkled mountains to the north. So far, the probability of a hidden threat looked small, but looks were often deceiving. Trench called Big Wally over.

"Any idea where we are?" he asked.

"Sure. We're at the MX silo complex at the north face of Sandstone Bluffs, about a mile from where I found the abandoned entrance to the MX installation. With any luck, my wheels will still be where I parked them."

"Okay," Trench returned. "We're moving out." They left the poured-concrete blockhouse, trudging through the high dune of windblown sand that had piled up around it.

Suddenly Phoenix saw the flash from beyond the deserted installation's perimeter, signaling an incoming projectile.

"Hit the dirt!" he screamed as the world exploded around him in a blaze of fire.

22

The SCORF hardguy in the camo-patterned HUMMER flung the smoking plastic firing tube of the LAW rocket to the ground and grabbed another on the double. Concentrated machine-gun fire from the M-60 mounted at the HUMMER's rear raked the low outcropping of rock behind which the targets had taken cover.

The desert rat patrol had been stationed at the access point to the underground complex with orders to shoot on sight. That's just what they did. It looked like there were two kills scored.

"It's a SCORF patrol," Trench told Big Wally.

"Two of the clones are dead. Two others are wounded and in shock," the little guy returned. "What's our next move?"

"Take the HUMMER. We need wheels." Trench consulted his chronometer. "They probably radioed for reinforcements. That gives us five minutes."

Trench told the surviving clones to take up positions to concentrate diversionary autofire on the HUMMER. He knew they wouldn't be able to hit the broad side of a barn, but he hoped the fire would keep the opposition focused on them when he made his play.

A line of red tracers streaked through the air, chewing up the sand in an arc of destruction aimed at the clones. Before the M-60 machine-gunner could get their range accurately, Trench broke from cover and pitched a stun grenade overhand at the HUMMER.

Two rapid *thuks* and the driver and radioman did spastic somersaults from the sides of the all-terrain military vehicle. Their bodies crashed and rolled, then were still with broken spines.

Autofire from Big Wally's Steyr AUG assault weapon blew them into whatever eternity was reserved for the Dark Messiah's mercs.

But the machine-gunner was still chattering away from the HUMMER's rear.

He'd taken out the clones quickly. Now he swung the deadly MG in the direction of Phoenix and Big Wally.

Each broke for open ground as flame belched from the M-60's muzzle and a stream of hellfire stitched the ground with dotted lines between their rolling bodies. The gunner couldn't decide which target to go for first. He swung the long black barrel at the big guy.

Wrong move.

Trench ducked and whirled, anticipating the gunner's choice. Coming out of his roll, he lobbed another stun grenade, taking out the machine-gunner. The SCORF guy's body split in three directions. Part of it was still attached to the MG that flopped muzzle-downward on its gimbal mountings.

"You okay?" Trench called to Big Wally. The midget looked like he might have been hit. He got up shakily and flashed Trench the thumbs-up signal, running to retrieve the AUG he'd dropped while running from the line of fire. He limped slightly on his way back.

"Just a sprain," the little guy said. "I'll live."

"Think you can drive?"

Big Wally nodded.

"That's good," returned Trench. " 'Cause we gotta leave in a hurry." He jerked his head in the direction of a rapidly approaching squad of HUMMERS.

"Looks like the cavalry just came riding in."

"With six-guns blazing."

"You got it, runt."

A blip on the radar screen in the mobile ADATS unit on the outskirts of Vegas alerted the tech. John Tallon looked over the tech's shoulder at the slowly moving pinpoint of green light on a black background.

"Sir," the tech informed the merc honcho. "The HUMMER's moving."

"Good," Tallon returned. "Inform Patrol Two to move into position."

Everything was going as smooth as silk. Trench and the midget had taken out the shave-tail recruits he'd stationed at the access ports to the abandoned MX missile facility. Tallon had figured Trench would want transportation out of the strike zone and had obligingly provided it in the form of HUMMERS he knew the Phung Hoang could take away from his pushover mercs as easily as pennies from a blind man's cup.

Unknown ᵥto Tallon's merc throwaways, though, the HUMMERS had been specially prepared with a plastique charge that would stop them in their tracks at Tallon's signal to the backup merc squad he'd deployed behind his first assault wave.

The guys coming in from behind weren't green. They were experts. They would stay just far enough away to keep out of MG range but close enough to make the lead HUMMER go exactly where they wanted it to go.

Tallon knew he was going out on a king-sized limb with the gamble he was taking. It would have been easier to just flood the subterranean scumhole of those Earthwomb freaks with one of the toxic nerve gases in his weapons arsenal. Or deply Cobra copters equipped with heat-seeking SIDEWINDER missiles to blow the targets straight to hell.

But the merc had a point to prove. More importantly, he had a score to settle. The Phung Hoang had displayed more luck than any man had a right to expect. Up till now, that is. But the Phoenix man's luck was bound to run out. And Tallon was going to exploit what the laws of probability told him was inevitable.

Trench and the midget didn't know it, but they were on a head-on collision course with the Angel of Death.

Here's where the soup started sticking to the spoon.

"Go!"

In the lead HUMMER, the SCORF trooper hit a stud on a remote radio-control unit detonating two shaped plastique charges behind the wheels of the fleeing vehicle just ahead. The charges would be enough to crack the axles in two but produce no more extensive damage than that.

The fleeing HUMMER's rear tires blew to smithereens as the charges snapped the front and rear axles like breadsticks. Big Wally fought to keep control of the crazily fishtailing vehicle, which skidded in the dust and crashed into a roadside boulder.

"Goddamnit!" Bit Wally swore. "Of all the bad luck."

"I wonder if that was luck," Trench told him, glancing behind them. The three-car patrol had slowed to a halt. Dead still, they appeared as though they were waiting for something to happen.

Just ahead was the Nevada ghost town called Hell Creek. It was either a trap or simply a coincidence. Trench didn't believe in coincidences when it came to combat.

It just didn't go down that way. Whether or not they'd been sandbagged, though, they'd have to make a stand. And the town was the only cover available.

Grabbing their weapons, ammo, and military ordnance taken from the MX underground complex's weapons-supply room, Trench and Big Wally beelined it across the blazing Mojave sands into the ghost town.

Hell Creek had been abandoned in 1912 when its rich lodes of silver, gold, and lead ore had petered out. All that was left were a cluster of ramshackle wooden buildings from which the paint had long since faded to a faint, almost colorless wash. The wood was cracked and blistered by the desert sun, but the dry Mojave desert air had preserved the structures otherwise completely intact.

Trench and Big Wally walked down Hell Creek's main street. To their right was a saloon, its doors flapping in the wind that blew tumbleweed across the unpaved thoroughfare. The left side of the street had an abandoned blacksmith's shop, complete with the rusted iron forge and anvil out front.

Further on, they could discern the sheriff's and assayers offices as well as another saloon in a building larger than the one nearest them with an empty wooden watering trough before the hitching post in front. A sign out front read, "Hard Luck."

A gust of hot desert wind, blowing through the ghost town with an eerie wail, kicked up a cloud of dust that swirled through the street, making the ancient signs creak on their hinges and sending tumbleweed rolling into an empty watering trough.

When the dust cleared, there were four blacksuited figures visible at the top of Hell Creek's main street.

It didn't take a rush of brains to figure out they'd been bushwhacked.

There was going to be a full-auto firefight on the main street of a ghost town in the middle of the Mojave Desert that hadn't seen a shotout in nearly one hundred years.

"Know what?" Big Wally asked.

Trench shook his head.

"Somehow, Toto, I don't think we're in Kansas anymore."

23

Steel-jacketed headbusters slammed into the hardpacked earth with the shrill deathsong of heavy-caliber autofire. The coordinated SMG capture bursts would have scored an immediate double burn if Trench hadn't shoved Big Wally out of the fire zone an instant before twin flames spouted from the hips of the four SCORF fast-gunners.

Some sixth sense had warned Phoenix that these mercs in black action-suits weren't throwaways like the cardboard mercs they'd encountered at the MX base access port. Their pinpoint shooting accuracy from the extreme limits of SMG firing range confirmed his premonition.

They were hunter-killers.

Tallon's killers. Somewhere, the Dark Messiah's Mauser-toting enforcer was bunkered down in a high-tech battle crib, directing the firefight from a safe distance like the gutless chickenshit he was, while his merc pawns did all the killing and all the dying.

It was clear to Phoenix that Tallon had

intended Hell Creek to be his graveyard. The
merc derived a perverted thrill from putting
things in boxes and watching them die. At the
SCORF Presidio hardbase in San Francisco,
Tallon had fed hacked-off human ears to starving
piranha he'd kept in a tank, and fed human beings
to terminal Contams driven to insane feeding
frenzies in a concrete pit.

Hell Creek was a box of a different kind, but a
box nonetheless. Tallon's scum mercs would be
hand-picked and personally trained with a single
objective in mind: to make goddamn sure that
Phoenix never left the ghost town alive.

Snapping off a blindfire SMG quickburst to
cover his sprint across the town's main street to
Big Wally's position, Trench ventured a glance in
the opposition's direction. The merc foursome
was gone. The subgun-wielding slayers had
broken for cover after firing their full-auto salvo.
It was clear they had played their opening gambit
as a psyche-out rather than a snuff-out.

Trench told Big Wally to stay put. This was
his fight. The little guy, fast and tricky though he
might be, was no match for the kind of lethal
weapons-masters these dudes undoubtedly were.
They'd burn the runt faster than a Dixie cup in a
firestorm.

Even if they took out Phoenix, the midget
still stood a chance. Odds were that Tallon's
HUMMERized goon crew sitting it out in the
desert like a flock of vultures would give up and
go home if the snuff team scored a takedown.

The key word was *if*. Phoenix wasn't about to
let that happen.

The merc slaughterers might have struck the
opening chord, but the deadly symphony was just
beginning. Phoenix palmed a fresh 40-round clip
of 185-grain JHPs into the MINIMI MG and

cocked the breech bolt on his MAC 11 SMG,
filling its chamber with a 9-mm high-performance
silvertip wadcutter.

A quick sequence of evasive fake-outs
brought Phoenix safely across the main street.
Big Wally watched Trench edge along the wall of
the tumbledown saloon with the MINIMI Megastopper in a two-handed carrying stance, ready
for instant deployment.

Before disappearing around the corner of the
saloon, Phoenix flashed the little guy the
thumb's-up high sign. Big Wally returned the
gesture. And then Phoenix was gone.

"Good luck, pard." He spoke in a soft voice.
The way you do when you've just lost a friend.
Then he cranked a round into his AUG and
hunkered down to wait out the firefight, hoping
against all logic that Phoenix would somehow
survive the lethal confrontation.

Deathlock and Quicksilver had blended into
the scenery after firing the diversionary 9-mm
longburst. As anticipated, the two targets had
split up. Only the primary target, designated
Phoenix, was of strategic significance. He was to
be considered extremely dangerous and
terminated with extreme prejudice. The
secondary target was a throwaway, to be burned
only if circumstances warranted the takedown.

Using hand signals to communicate silently
as they stalked their human prey, the SCORF
deathbringers moved through the eerily deserted
streets of the Nevadan ghost town.

Trained specifically for this precise combat
environment over a period of many long months
at the SCORF hardbase in the Blue Mountains
Clear Zone using a full-scale mockup and live
targets, the merc slaymasters of Operation Pact

of Steel now felt the adrenalin-fed rush of manic exhilaration that only going into a firefight produced.

Their target may have been only a single man, yet each of the mercs was aware of how highly dangerous this particular man was. They had been fully briefed by Tallon on Phoenix's one-man guerilla war in nuke-torn San Francisco. Their incredible intel was that Phoenix had singlehandedly used low-yield subkiloton nukes to wipe out an entire SCORF army in the Urban Containment Zone.

Although they had only tantalizing rumors to provide reasons why Phoenix was so hotly sought after, they knew it had something to do with the Soviet supervirus called the Plague.

This man held the key to stopping the incurable mutation-causing disease.

Possibly what impressed them most about their deadly quarry was the information provided them concerning Phoenix's activities in Vietnam as a member of the legendary Long-Range Patrol (LURP) Special Operations Group. Tallon's mercs hadn't even learned to jerk off when Nam was a firezone. Never having known real combat and knowing that Magnus Trench had survived the Southeast Asian meatgrinder had given them all massive inferiority complexes. They had plenty of training, sure, but not a hell of a lot more than that.

Yeah, there were SCORF raids against the Aliens down in the Hotzones to the south, population-control operations in the Urban Containment Zones, and skirmishes along the Alaskan War Frontier with SinoSov shock troops. But there had never been a full-scale land war for them to prove their manhood.

Drugs and hypnotherapy at the Blue

Mountains hardbase had taken this insecurity and blown it up into a deep psychotic motivation to waste the target at all costs. Tallon's windup mercs were programmed to kill, even at the expense of their own lives.

Quicksilver signaled to Deathlock to cover him as he prepared to cross the space between two buildings, a move that would bring him out into the open long enough for a 9-mm burst to frag him to bloody hamburger if he weren't agile, mobile, and hostile.

Deathlock nodded and Quicksilver darted from cover, the muzzle of his SMG waving back and forth like some obscene insect's probing antenna as he executed a series of coordinated dodgeback body fakes to throw off a gunner's bead.

The merc duo was performing just like the pros Trench had assumed they would be. Only they weren't as good as they thought. Despite their outward professionalism, the fastgunning mercs had missed Phoenix watching them from his flat-lying vantage point atop the roof of the hotel directly beside them.

Pulling a Hush-Puppy-type silencer taken from the MX installation's weapons room from a canvas pouch on his belt, Trench threaded it into the muzzle of the MAC 11 SMG and aimed just ahead of the merc duo as they crouch-walked down the street. Phoenix was going to do some "shepherding" of his own.

Whispering autofire made debris geyser as Trench walked his fire toward the blacksuited combo, instantly sending the two mercs diving into the doorway of the saloon directly to their right, where they frantically jerked their heads trying to pinpoint the origin of the flash-suppressed, silenced autoburst that had seemingly come directly up from the brown dirt beneath their feet.

A second quickburst sent the mercs high-tailing it into the saloon. Phoenix smiled grimly. That was exactly where Trench wanted them to go.

Inside the saloon, a Hogan's Alley awaited his two lethal playmates.

In Nam, the LURPS had fine-tuned the Hogan's Alley technique to an art form in man-killing. It had worked well for Trench and the Genesis crew in Frisco. Now, Phoenix used a variation on the technique, deploying the claymore remote antipersonnel mines taken from the MX-missile underground hardbase's security arsenal. The claymores had been placed at strategic intervals designed to bounce the suckers around like ping-pong balls.

Silently climbing from his rooftop vantage point, Trench whipped the compact remote unit from his pack. A series of rapid concussions erupted from within the abandoned saloon as he hit the detonator button. Autofire ratcheted as one of the hardguys came running out, firing wildly as smoke rose from his soot-stained black-suit, his crazed brain reacting to the images of his partner being blown to bloody smithereens by the explosives Trench had placed in the booby-trapped saloon.

Deathlock's features were contorted in a grimace of numbing shock and surprise as he suddenly focused on the grim-visaged apparition standing in front of him. *Where had the guy come from?* One second there was only thin air between him and the building across the street and now he was face-to-face with the Angel of Death, his reaper's scythe replaced with a huge black machine gun.

He'd just seen Quicksilver's body ripped to shreds as concussion rings tore the arms and legs from his torso and blasted gobbits of his kidneys, lungs, and heart all over the place.

No! The guy *wasn't* standing there. He *couldn't* be standing there. No matter how good he was, there was no fucking way a guy just walked out of nowhere. It was shock that was making Deathlock hallucinate. He'd prove it by blasting a few dozen holes right through the evilly grinning mirage.

The merc raised his JATI to fire.

Before he could level its muzzle, the subgun was seized by an incredibly powerful hand.

The hand tore the JATI SMG from Deathlock's grasp as though taking a rattle from an infant.

Stunned, the merc watched the big guy smoothly eject the subgun's 32-round magazine and thumb out the 9-mm roundnose bullets slug by slug, then casually fling the empty SMG to the dirt.

Deathlock quickly drew a wickedly serrated nine-inch MALIN-MK survival knife from a fast-whip scabbard on his thigh. His knife hand feinted back and forth in an intricate series of figure-eight snake moves that cleaved through the air with a loud ugly whistle while Deathlock crouched and beckoned Trench with his free hand to come on in and party.

A vicious smile played across his lips as he taunted the man who had killed his hard pard before moving into an underhand death swipe.

"There won't be enough left of you to wipe on a Kleenex, candyass," the merc snarled. "I'm gonna slice you up, cocksucker."

Before the merc's sneer had time to fade,

Deathlock's knife and the hand clutching it was dissolved by a 9-mm fragburst from a MAC 11 SMG. Deathlock stared at the blood spewing from the slashed arteries in the amputated stump in utter disbelief, then at the smoking barrel of the Ingram SMG in the big man's hand.

Nobody could be that fast! he thought.

But then all mental activity was replaced by a searing agony that made the merc sink to his knees, howling dementedly in pain.

A fast headshot solved Deathlock's problems quickly and permanently, cleanly decapitating the merc and sending the headless corpse toppling forward into the blood-soaked ground.

Trench Warfare sprinted from the execution site. Backup would be coming in fast and heavy. Trench knew this with a cold, brutal certainty. How large and how hard the big SCORF chill would come down was anybody's guess, but Phoenix figured the dues-paying would be of epic proportions.

He wasn't wrong.

Saggitar and Moebius weren't taking chances. Deathlock and Quicksilver had been hair-trigger hotheads, cowboys who were strictly gun and run. Cool-headed and combat-toughened, the mercs in the second team had seen enough bloody street-fighting in the nuclear TDZs to know how to handle themselves with steel nerves and lightning-swift reflexes.

Saggitar and Moebius went strictly by the book, and the book said that the candyass punk target was already history.

Trench walked right into the merc ambush. Breaking from their concealed positions, the slay team cut loose with a wall of saturated autofire from opposite sides of the narrow cross streets. Though Trench would have liked to avoid the potential deathtrap of taking cover in one of the surrounding buildings that were little more than piles of kindling awaiting a spark to set them off, the withering lead cross-hail forced him to move fast for the safety of the nearest structure.

It was the other old saloon. The bar still fronted an antique mirror against the broken slat-and-plaster wall. Some cobwebbed tables stood on a floor thick with yellow desert dust and wind-blown tumbleweed. Taking up positions outside the door, the merc teams hosed the saloon down with concentrated autofire, reducing the mirror to a fountain of exploding glass as Trench dove low and fast behind the bar.

Moebius and Saggitar had Phoenix where they wanted him. They wouldn't risk going in, cowboying it like Deathlock and Quicksilver. Their quarry wasn't going anywhere except hell. With a third team, Fast Dancer and Bloodstone, bracketing the building's rear, Phoenix was as good as dead and buried. Again, the book dictated what they'd do next.

Moebius and Saggitar whipped out HK grenade-launching pistols and assumed firing positions. Propping the retractable metal buttstocks on their thighs they fired from a crouching position.

Four near-simultaneous concussions erupted where the incendiary cylinders impacted and exploded. A red-orange fireball consumed the ancient ginmill in a boiling inferno.

The members of the SCORF kill crew shaded their eyes from the searing heat of the raging firestorm, knowing nothing within could survive. All that would be left of the target, code-named Phoenix, would be a cloud of scattered ashes on the wind.

Ashes from which this Phoenix would never rise again. Not in a million years. Not in a billion lifetimes.

24

Death howled above him, clawing at the sky with talons of flame.

Even in the depths of the abandoned storm cellar that lay beneath the Hard Luck Saloon, Trench could feel the firestorm's intense heat and hear the thunderclaps produced by cooler air rushing in to fill the vacuum produced by the inferno as the building above him went up in a ball of flame.

Had he not seen the trap door, silted over by decades-worth of fine, windblown desert dust, Phoenix would have been incinerated where he had stood.

Lighting a flare, Trench made a fast recon of the storm cellar. It had been cleaned out decades ago. Nothing was left but a few worm-eaten pieces of furniture and some empty crates on a dirt floor. But there was another way out.

Behind a barrel was a crudely planked-up hole in the saloon's brick foundation wall. A couple of whacks with the MINIMI's solid-metal buttstock and the rotted planks splintered into a thousand toothpick-sized fragments. Beyond the jagged hole in the foundation bricks his flare revealed a narrow tunnel, barely large enough for a man to crawl through on hands and knees, unless he had a very good reason.

Trench had the best—*staying alive*.

Choking black smoke from the burning building above him was already flooding the cellar and flaming pieces of wood from the burning floor overhead were raining down into the pit below. A cave-in was imminent. Another few seconds and the storm cellar would become a deathtrap as the entire floor came crashing down in a fiery avalanche.

Digging his nails into the cool, soft dirt of the tunnel floor, Trench clawed and kicked his way through the claustrophobic passageway that ran for several hundred yards in pitch-darkness.

The tunnel ended in a trapdoor set in the floor planking of the mayor's office across the street. From its large rectangular window, Trench had a diagonal view of the backs of the merc foursome that watched the flames consume the saloon.

The maggots from SCORF were dead, even though they didn't know it yet.

With two fistfuls of MINIMI stopping power, Phoenix fast-sprinted from the Hell Creek mayor's office into the street.

The mercs whirled at the sound of motion behind them. Though speechless with shock at the sight of the living being they thought was already a pile of cinders, they came up grabbing metal anyway. Combat reflexes overrode mute fear, jerking the trigger fingers on rapidly deployed SMGs set in full-auto firing modes.

Flame and lead exploded like the hot breath of the death god as the MINIMI belched out a hellfire hurricane of SS109 62-grain penetrator bullets.

Moebius and Saggitar clownishly threw up

their arms and stuck out their legs in weird sitting positions as a steel-jacketed autofire longburst hurled them ten feet into the air and sent them crashing back to earth again like profane marionettes, their mangled, twisted bodies leaking blood from gaping multiple-entry wounds and their assault weapons lying uselessly in the dirt beside them.

Phoenix did a half-somersault out of the line of fire as the two merc survivors of Operation Pact of Steel opened up with everything they had, then broke and ran, blindfiring over their shoulders. Quickbursts from Trench's lead-squirting MINIMI M249 MG tore up the street as the scum duo jackrabbited for whatever cover they could find.

Phoenix pursued Fast Dancer and Blood-stone into the town assayer's office. The mercs were scared. Outgunned and outmaneuvered by a one-man execution squad, they had gone over the edge into screaming insanity.

They were deadmen and they knew it.

No ordinary human being could have survived the blazing funeral pyre the incendiary grenades had made of the saloon. The man called Phoenix . . . *was* a Phoenix.

Nothing fazed this supermerc. He walked through fire as though it weren't even there.

They felt like turning around and flinging themselves at his high-booted feet, begging him to spare their lives. Only the suspicion that Phoenix would have just blown them away without a second thought prevented them.

Steel-jacketed wadcutters Swiss-cheesed the wood of the overturned hardwood table they'd barricaded themselves behind, driving knife-edged splinters into Fast Dancer's face. Blood trickled down his forehead from multiple skin cuts.

Bloodstone unclipped a Stingball M452C antipersonnel grenade and armed the black-metal ball filled with marble-sized steel shot by pulling the cotter pin set in its conical head. Waiting until the sound of autofire stopped, Bloodstone dodged from cover and prepared to pitch the grenade sidearmed.

"Suck this, mother f—"

The black handle of an expertly thrown K-BAR combat knife magically appeared in the upper right of the merc's abdominal region as the nine-inch serrated-steel blade sliced through muscles, arteries, and internal organs before his brain could order his arm to hurl the grenade or his fingers to drop it.

Bloodstone froze in terminal shock, unable to decide whether to put his hands on the blood-fountaining stomach wound or let the grenade fly.

The grenade made up his mind for him.

An explosion tore the merc's arm off at the elbow and lifted the scum cowboy off his feet in a reverse somersault like a trapeze artist with a death wish.

Phoenix had just made the commando's wish come true.

His one-way ticket to hell, courtesy of Phoenix, landed him across a table with his intestines bursting out of the red hamburger of his massive stomach wound like gigantic bloodworms. The merc flopped off the table and landed belly-up on the dusty floor. Tonight, the SCORF fastgunner would serve dinner to Hell Creek's rat population.

In the last remaining seconds of his life, the merc who had been programmed to believe that he was the baddest of the bad was reduced to a pathetic human cockroach, covered with his own blood, shit, and vomit as he crawled across the floor and went into agonized convulsions while his dying brain overloaded his nerves with a haywire assortment of motor commands.

Phoenix put the dying merc to sleep forever. His MAC SMG spoke its fiery last rites and the merc became an angel. Borne on the wings of death, Bloodstone's organs splattered from his corpse in a river of red as he flew through the air.

Only this angel never reached heaven. He was on a one-way trip to hell. The mutilated remains flopped over a long, cobwebbed table that ran the length of one side of the large room. The legs scissored once, then the body went limp and slid to the floor, ending up face-down in the desert dust.

"*Goddamn you!*" Fast Dancer screamed as he cut loose with an SMG burst that was blind, wild, and poorly configured.

"You're not fucking human! You're not for real!"

In his panic, confusion, and fear, Fast Dancer's psychochemically induced hatred of the target overcame his instinct for survival. The odds weren't fair. Tallon had sent him and the others up against something more than human. The crew had never stood a chance. They were good, yeah—against other human beings they were good.

But this was no ordinary man they were facing.

This dude was pure fucking hell.

At that moment, Fast Dancer realized that they had all been set up.

Tallon was using them as throwaways to soften up this supermerc. He had to be. There was no other explanation.

Fast Dancer realized that his seconds were numbered. He only hoped that the backup Tallon had waiting in the wings would nail the Phoenix scumbag right to the wall.

The merc ducked behind an overturned hardwood table and got off his last remaining rounds in a cover-fire quickburst.

Fast Dancer's cover fire gave him enough seconds to crash through the picture window of the assayer's office, doing a tight somersault that landed him on his feet. As he hit the ground running, he knew he'd bought himself some time.

Although his move was prompted by blind panic, it nevertheless kept Fast Dancer a lifebeat away from being cut down by the line of concentrated MINIMI autofire as Phoenix stood in the shattered window and shot from the hip.

Fast Dancer zigzagged through the ghost town's dirt streets, firing over his shoulder as he ran for his life. He panted as he leaned against the side of a clapboard building, catching his breath. The merc was so wired he didn't even notice that he'd been hit in the thigh by a ricocheted slug fragment from the MINIMI firestorm.

Maybe he had a chance after all. Maybe this dude wasn't as slick as he was cracked up to be. Fast Dancer's courage was returning. He was the cream. He was the best.

He'd fast-track the opposition and leave the bozo a gutter-sucking corpse.

But adrenalin and courage were two different things. Fast Dancer was pumped full of the former and had none of the latter. Riding high on his own fear-juice, he was unaware of the dark trail of blood from a thigh wound that followed him through the dust-caked streets.

Phoenix was, though.

It was only a matter of seconds before he'd have a clear shot at a fast takedown. Trench waited. In combat, patience paid off.

Forged in the steaming jungles of Southeast Asia, Phoenix's combat senses were on full alert as he waited for his quarry to move. He had become a big cat, hunting for man-meat. He sensed rather than knew, acted rather than thought. He was tuned to the vibrations of his prey as surely as any tiger prowling in its natural habitat.

Fast Dancer gulped air and prepared to move from cover. Holding the SMG in a two-handed combat grip he got ready to lunge around the corner, firing as he ran.

A powerful hand crashed through the wall behind him. Steel fingers locked around the merc's neck in an unbreakable grip.

The hand pulled Fast Dancer right through the flimsy wall. As easily as pulling a doll through a cardboard box.

The Grim Reaper stared at Fast Dancer through merciless eyes.

Trench looked down at the kneeling merc. Turning, he walked away. He hoped the punk wouldn't try to off him. Phoenix was giving him a chance to live. But he knew the kind Tallon's mercs were. SCORF, the NCSC's Special Commando Relatiatory Force, wouldn't have accepted anything with a heart, soul, or conscience.

And if they had, those qualities would have been peeled away, layer by layer, like the skin of an onion, until they could effortlessly mold the psyche at the merc's core into any shape they pleased.

By killing the punk, Phoenix knew he'd be doing him the favor of his life.

Fast Dancer fought the impulse to vomit which was tying his stomach into painful knots. But he had enough strength left to pick up his JATI SMG from where the weapon had fallen on the floor of the abandoned Hell Creek general store.

His every survival instinct told him to cool it,

to hold back, that he couldn't carry the play, even with the guy showing him his back.

But his SCORF mindfucking, his naked greed, his berserk cowboy mentality—twisted and deformed by SCORF brainwashing techs until it had been programmed like some lethal computer chip—made Fast Dancer lift the JATI in quaking hands and aim it at the small of Trench's back.

"Life's a bitch. . . ." he began to say.

Before he could pull the trigger a light shone.

It was a light that he knew opened the gates to heaven.

The light shone from the mouth of the MAC 11 SMG in Trench's fist. The light bored its way into Fast Dancer's chest like a white-hot lance, impaling the merc like an insect on a glittering pin.

"And then you die," Trench finished for the merc. He pulled the MAC's trigger again, once more turning on the lethal light.

Fast Dancer coughed, spitting up chunks of red lung tissue. The merc sat down against a wall, his eyes rolling up in his head.

"T-Tallon . . ." he was able to whisper with his dying breath. "You're finished, sucker." The merc smiled a blood-dripping smile and shivered as his heart stopped beating.

Trench reholstered the MAC at his side as Fast Dancer's head sagged to the dead merc's body and the corpse slid along the wall, leaving a dark swath of blood behind it.

"Rest in peace," Phoenix said, adding as an afterthought, "Candyass."

He walked out into the bright desert sun, smelling the odor of the burning ghost town.

Straight into the shadow that had fallen across his life. Like the image of a gravestone.

Tallon was about to call in his final play.

25

"*Daddy!*"

Brian Trench called to his father from the other end of the sunbaked main street of Hell Creek, Nevada. Clutching the boy's hand was his wife Sandra. Lines of pain and confusion etched her pretty face, turning it into a mask of terror.

"Go back, Trench!" she screamed. "They want to kill you! Don't come near us! Run, goddamnit!"

SCORF troopers in space-helmeted SCICON combat suits that gave them the appearance of alien astronauts trained deadly Valmet AK .308 assault weapons on Trench's wife and young son.

Magnus Trench's brain reeled at the shock of seeing his family. Every survival instinct told him they could not really be there before his eyes. Warning alarms were sounding furiously in his mind.

SCORF was capable of anything, and using exact doubles as bait for entrapment was a trick as old as they come. Except it would have been practically impossible for Tallon to compile enough data on his wife and child to locate their duplicates—Trench doubted if such information existed even in the EMP-hardened supercomputers available to SCORF, and only a miracle too incredible to believe possible could have preserved personal photos from nuclear incineration in the Trench family's Manhattan apartment.

"Trench!" The voice booming out over the HUMMER-mounted public-address system belonged to the merc named Tallon. Trench recognized it immediately. Once you heard it, it was a voice you never forgot. "Throw down your weapons. We have your wife and child. Surrender and they won't be harmed.

"Fire on us and we'll snuff your family, Phung Hoang."

Trench had zero options. He now understood that Tallon had considered the SCORF hit crew expendable from the git-go. Fast Dancer had alerted him with his final taunt.

John Tallon had an ace in the hole.

An offer that Phoenix couldn't refuse. The one-in-a-million possibility that SCORF had located his family and now held them prisoner was impossible to dismiss.

Breaking from cover, Trench stepped warily out into the main street of Hell Creek, holding the MINIMI ready for a full-auto capture burst to cover his dash for cover.

It was Sandra and Brian. It *had* to be them. He recognized the T-shirt his son had on as the one he'd worn when his family had seen him off on the business trip to San Francisco that had for Trench, and two hundred million other Americans, preceded the start of a nuclear nightmare.

Trench measured his wife's face and voice against the image and soundtrack in his brain and found a perfect match. Yes, it was really Sandra. Against all odds his wife and his son were now only a few hundred yards from him.

The sole object of his struggle to survive in the post-nuke hellworld had been to be reunited with his family, if they survived. And their survival and the form it took had been a source of constant torment to Trench in long, desperate months since the nuclear mushrooms rose skyward, incinerating everything they touched. He ached to run to them, to touch them.

In Trench's mind, there was no other alternative but to play Tallon's game.

Tallon had saved Sandra and Brian as his ace in the hole, Trench knew. If the merc couldn't corral him one way, he'd corral him another. The merc psycho had skillfully exploited the concern for his loved ones that had been keeping Trench on tenterhooks for months. Could SCORF have located his family, even in the radioactive ruins of New York City?

The answer now was *yes*. It was certain, since the Dark Messiah had discovered that Trench was a walking production center and storehouse for the Alpha-Immune antibodies to the Plague supervirus—antibodies which could save the Messiah's life in a bone-marrow implant—that every resource of the US-NCSC Government controlled by Luther Enoch had been put on priority alert to discover their whereabouts and capture them if they were still alive. The leverage over Phoenix that holding his wife and son prisoner would give SCORF would be incalculable.

And with that answer, Trench knew that Tallon and Enoch had him signed, sealed, and practically delivered. Without his family, survival held no meaning for him. If there were even the slightest chance that Tallon would allow them to live, Phoenix had no alternative but to surrender.

Trench threw down the MINIMI M249. The light machine gun struck the ground with a solid thud. The rest of his weapons followed.

"That's the right move," came Tallon's voice over the public-address. "Now walk slowly forward. With your hands over your head."

SCORF troopers immediately surrounded him. Phoenix became the eye of a hurricane of bristling gun barrels. Using metal detectors and CAM sniffers to ascertain that he carried no concealed weapons or explosives, Tallon's mercs expertly frisked him.

"Okay," Tallon said again through the public-address. "I'm satisfied. Bring him over here."

Phoenix was taken at subgun-point to his wife and children a few yards away.

"You three deserve a reunion," Tallon said. "Go on, honey, put your arms around hubby there. You too, junior."

Sandra and Brian ran to Trench. Their arms reached out to touch him.

The two bodies seemed to slow as they ran with their legs in midair.

Squares of digital color replaced the firm contours of living bodies.

The squares became whirling motes as the two-dimensional bodies dissolved into nothingness.

"Holographic constructs," Tallon explained. "Lifelike but, unfortunately, not the real thing, Phung Hoang."

Phoenix had walked in leading with his chin.

Tallon smiled.

"To paraphrase an old song, 'You're so mystifyingly sad, I'm Dr. Dying Glad.' "

Tallon leveled an ugly, long-barreled black handgun and fired point-blank into his target's chest. Magnus Trench was knocked backward by

the projectile's impact. Darkness quickly overcame him.

"Take the body away," Tallon barked at the
SCICON-suited SCORF troopers awaiting his
orders. "There's a C-5B transport waiting at the
airport outside Vegas. Your Dark Messiah wants
it delivered fast."

EPILOGUE

Big Wally hung his head and listened to the crackling of the flames that had spread from the burning Hard Luck Saloon to set the rest of Hell Creek ablaze.

This time, he knew, there wasn't a damned thing he could do. Tallon had the big guy dead-bang.

He watched as the SCORF crew loaded the limp, deathlike body of Magnus Trench into the AH-64 gunship and the big, heavily armed copter lifted off the desert landing zone.

Before too long nothing would be left of Hell Creek, Nevada, but a few heaps of smoldering wreckage and a lot of bad memories.

Nothing left but ashes.

The little big man knew the motorized SCORF patrol that had been stationed on the highway would be gone. Nobody would be interested in the minnow once they'd caught the whale. It would be a long, hot walk to his pickup, but Big Wally would make it.

He wished the Lone Ranger would rest in peace.

The little guy would remember Phoenix. For a long time to come.

Big Wally slung the Steyr AUG .223 assault weapon over his shoulder and began walking down the blacktop ribbon toward the distant, glittering fairyland that shimmered in the midday heat. A fairyland called Las Vegas.

CLASSIFIED: TOP SECRET
OPERATIONAL URGENT

FR LAS VEGAS NV/TALLON
TO BIG STONE GAP/ENOCH 387Q#6

OPERATION PACT OF STEEL EXECUTED X ENTIRE SPECIAL OPS GROUP SUFFERED FATAL CASUALTIES FOLLOWING PITCHED FIREFIGHT IN GHOST TOWN OF HELL CREEK NV X COMPUTER GENERATED HOLOGRAM USED TO BRING TARGET DESIGNATE PHOENIX INTO CAPTURE POSITION X TARGET DESIGNATE PHOENIX NEUTRALIZED BY GAS PROPELLED INJECTION OF CHLORAMPHENICOL ADRENOCORTICOID CAUSING INSTANTANTEOUS LOSS OF CONSCIOUSNESS AND TOTAL IMMOBIL- IZATION X TARGET DESIGNATE PHOENIX CURRENTLY IN-FLIGHT ABOARD C-5B TRANSPORT AIRCRAFT DESIGNATED MANDARIN EN ROUTE TO ANDREWS AFB TRANSFERRAL TO BIG STONE GAP HARDBASE X ETA TWO HUNDRED HOURS

ACKNOWLEDGE AND CONFIRM

BT
9870#2
EOM